Speak, Adam

Twentieth Century Scottish Women's Fiction
Series Editor: Anne McManus Scriven

Speak, Adam
Moira Burgess

Kennedy & Boyd

Kennedy & Boyd
an imprint of
Zeticula
57 St Vincent Crescent
Glasgow
G3 8NQ
Scotland

http://www.kennedyandboyd.co.uk
admin@kennedyandboyd.co.uk

First published as *A Rumour of Strangers*, in 1987,
ISBN 0-00-223107-7
This edition, with introduction, first published 2009
Copyright © Moira Burgess 1987, 2009
Introduction Copyright © Valentina Poggi 2009
Cover photograph © Colum Scriven 2009

ISBN-13 978 1 904999 63 8
ISBN-10   1 904999 63 8

For Kirsten and Peter

Introduction

'...a matchstick model town... a toy that you could hold in your hand.'

–Speak, Adam

This is what Finavay looks like, seen from above early in the novel, to its protagonist Christa Beresford, who used to go this small town on a Highland coast on her holidays as a child. Now, in her thirties, Christa has come back for good, to manage the boarding house she has inherited from her aunt; a move which, for her and her husband Billy, means saying farewell to their life in Glasgow. A half-stranger, if not quite a stranger to the town as he is, she will gradually come to realize that, contrary to her initial confident view, nearly everyone here harbours some mystery, some secret, just as nearly everyone regards them with contempt, suspicion, or downright hostility. Her tentative course toward mutual forbearance, if not familiarity and understanding, with the people who form the social chorus and lay down the moral law in Finavay, meets with more or less overt rebuffs, and by the end of the novel the couple, still incomers, will appear as far as ever from being integrated into the local society.

For all that, the novel does not lack a happy end. In the first place this is because by then Christa and Billy have got over a difficult moment in their still young married life, becoming closer than ever before. Their strengthened relationship is largely thanks to that very experience of alienation and isolation which has fostered in them a deeper consciousness of their love, and a generous need to protect each other from the malice of the self-enclosed community.

It is not only onto the lives of the protagonists – who arrive at Finavay, do their best to try and reach its vital centre, then give up the attempt but stay on, quietly holding by the right to live there on their own terms – that the author impresses this 'in-and-out' movement. It can be said to concern also the genre pattern of this novel in its revisiting of the archetypal images of village or small-town life as they are presented both in the original Kailyard tradition, and in its twentieth-century version, the so-called 'anti-Kailyard' that can be considered fundamentally specular to the other.[1] *Speak, Adam* assesses, counterpoints, and finally dismisses, both sub-generic modes as inadequate to express the variety of ways in which different people can respond to the pressures of scandal, censure, moral bear-baiting and scapegoat-making in small communities. But before analysing the novel's structure and themes as a way to explain this contention, some information about its author is in order.

Moira Burgess was born in 1936, and her first novel, *The Day Before Tomorrow*, appeared in 1971. At that time she worked as a professional librarian. In the same year she was awarded an M.A. from the University of Strathclyde, with a thesis published by the Scottish Library Association in 1972 under the title *The Glasgow Novel 1870-1970*, and then re-published, with substantial additions and integrations, in 1986 and again 1999.[2] In the interval Burgess had married and had two children, whom subsequently she was to bring up as a single parent. She left librarianship but wrote critical articles and did other scholarly work on Scottish literature: in 1985 she edited, with Hamish White, an anthology of short stories set in Glasgow, and two years later, by herself, another anthology of 19th and 20th century writing by Scottish women. [3] Both collections contained excellent selections of significant authors, many of them till then too little known or underrated. In 1982 a grant from the Scottish Arts Council encouraged Burgess to return to writing her own fiction and she published a number of short stories and in 1987 brought out this, her second novel, then called *A Rumour of Strangers*.

Of late Burgess has turned her critical interest to Naomi Mitchison: in 2006 she was awarded a PhD from Glasgow University for her thesis on the supernatural and mythical elements in the work of that extraordinary author; a book based on that thesis has now been published.[4] She is working on an edition of Mitchison's collected prose. For many years she was much in request for talks and lectures to writers' groups and at literary conferences, but now devotes herself mainly to her chief vocation of the writing of fiction, and has completed two dark Glasgow novellas and a novel set in the Western Isles.[5]

Glasgow and the West Highlands are obviously prominent locations in her writings, as they are in her life, since she was born in Campbeltown, Argyll, and lives and works in Glasgow. Both these pervasive elements in her imagination appear in *Speak, Adam*, though in unequal measure. The natural setting of the novel is the landscape of the West Highland coast, the sea and the birch wood where travelling tinkers recurrently camp and depart; its stable social milieu is a small-town population of housewives and shopkeepers, publicans and churchgoers, most of them devoted to scandal-mongering. In the background there lies always Glasgow, to whose welcoming bosom, in Billy's opinion, he and his wife could quickly flee back from the bother and chores of the big, damp, rambling boarding house, and from the malice of local gossip. Christa however does not cherish only happy memories of Glasgow, as it was there that Billy, a short time previous to their coming to Finavay, had got himself into trouble by seducing a schoolgirl.

Indeed, the name of Glasgow crops up at various times in the novel - now as that of a natural hiding place for a runaway country lass, now of temporary shelter for a disgraced victim of supposed rape. But the aura of sexual excess or sexual frustration does not hover solely around the big distant city:

it permeates even more deeply the atmosphere of Finavay itself, in a variety of shapes: frigidity and sterility of long-standing in marriage, adultery, mindless promiscuity, gloating curiosity and false prudishness, and, darker than all the rest, rage at sexual deprivation inflicted by early widowhood and vented not only into loveless sex, but into hatred and spite at other people's married happiness.

When Christa takes up her position as the mistress of Finavay's boarding house, and the boss of the supremely reliable housekeeper Ellen and the typical Highland maidservant Dolina, she has no inkling of all this. Her idea of Finavay at this stage would recall the benevolent if vaguely ironic village vignettes of Barrie and MacLaren, were it not that she appears disturbed by the presence of tinkers – ever the objects of her aunt's disgust – as well as by the sight of the middle-aged church elder and butcher Calum: the latter detail remains somewhat cryptic, probably a hint at some connection between that man and Christa's first insight, as a child, into the mystery of sexuality. However, long before Christa herself, the reader perceives that she lives in the midst of an anti-Kailyard model community, most of whose inhabitants do not resemble those of *A Window in Thrums*[6] or *Beside the Bonnie Briar Bush*,[7] but rather the bodies of Barbie[8] and the folk of Kinraddie;[9] unless a better term of comparison should be found in the less savage, though no less explicit anti-Kailyard villages of female fiction, like Shepherd's *Quarry Wood* and *Weatherhouse*,[10] or Kesson's *Glitter of Mica* and *Another Time, Another Place*.[11]

The parallel tensions, between locals and incomers and between sub-genres, one the distorting mirror of the other, are not of course the sole nor the principal themes and motives of interest in the novel. Its main narrative focus appears to be the psychosexual deadlock created for Christa and Billy by the recent birth of a stillborn child. Christa's distress, heightened by her guilt for having urged him to have intercourse with her at an advanced phase of the pregnancy, now makes her shrink more or less openly from her husband's advances, with the result of throwing him back for consolation and retaliation on his habits of drinking and philandering. This latter failing, its rankling memory and her belated jealousy also have a part in Christa's mixed-up state of mind: her body yearns for an embrace likely to renew the expectation of maternity, and at the same time she longs to punish Billy by her frigid attitude. The supposition of such a devious inner conflict is confirmed by the fact that finally Christa's revulsion from intimacy with her husband will suddenly disappear after her climactic sexual encounter with the tinker Adam. This momentary unpredictable experience - unsought for at least at a conscious level and satisfying only in the purely physical sense - is enough to enable guilt and anguish at frustrated motherhood fall away from Christa like a bad enchantment, leaving her free to seek a *rapprochement* with the husband she really loves.

The tinkers, especially the emblematic young male Adam, provide another significant focus in the novel. Characterized from the very start by their carefree and prolific sexuality, when Adam coming along with his pregnant wife leers at Christa unashamedly, they are subtly related both to the young woman's yearning for a new baby and to her memories of the past, when, as a little girl, she would be cautioned by her aunt to avoid the 'tinks' as persons dirty in body and mind. This view, still obviously prevalent in Finavay, is, if not explicitly denied, is at any rate ironically countermined by the contrast the reader is invited to establish between the sort of dirt imputed to them, and that which fills the prurient minds of all respectable people in Finavay, and the daily lives of most of them.

A symbol of this unwholesome moral atmosphere emerges, in the latter part of the novel, in the offensive smell that Christa perceives with growing disquiet in the kitchen of her still partly unexplored mansion. Its cause will prove to be gross disregard of basic hygienic norms and at the same time of moral and social conventions, and familiarity with a filth in comparison to which the reputed 'dirty habits' of the tinkers must appear cleanly and wholesome. This obnoxious odour, of close, secretive sex and eating, comes also to symbolize, or at least suggest, the basic vice of the anti-Kailyard social body of Finavay: its members are addicted to sweeping under the carpet of pretended ignorance those same transgressions – deteriorated marital relations, illicit affairs, true or pretended rapes, whoring – about which they gleefully whisper in daily gossip. The moment however they threaten to damage the good name of the community as a whole, these same gossiping tongues then unanimously turn to lay the blame on the 'strangers', the incomers and outsiders, whose presence has unconsciously disturbed the delicate network of antagonisms, the balance of mutual back-biting and complicity, that hold the local people together protecting the self-esteem of them all, (except maybe for people too naïve like young Finlay, or too vulnerable and disgraced like Flora Ferguson).

Before seeing how far Burgess really allows this extreme anti-Kailyard view of her village to go, I should like to note an interesting aspect of her narrative technique. With an adroitness worthy of an expert in thrillers, in the ten pages of the first chapter of her novel she scatters a number of clues about what is going to happen, dropping hints about her characters' past experiences and present difficulties: clues and hints sufficiently vague and subtle to arouse the curiosity of readers who later on can find themselves either gratified by seeing their surmises confirmed, or surprised by the sudden turn given their deceptive expectations, or else can be just left wondering. All the relevant elements in the story are, more or less casually, touched upon in the first chapter. The tinkers and Christa's complex attitude to them, her tense reaction to Billy's overtures (the effect not of frigidity but of a quivering awareness of her body's condition and needs), his impulse to seek relief elsewhere, Ellen's seeming aloofness, Dolina's precocious ambition to run a brothel, the still unlocated back door of the big house, the mention in one breath of two persons, nurse and butcher, by all appearance unrelated: all these are threads that in the following pages will prove related to one another like the filaments of a spider's web, hanging in a breeze of suspense. The suspense here is not, however, the lurid kind of thriller – a subgenre that Burgess seems bent rather on parodying, for instance when she leads her readers to anticipate a murder perpetrated behind the secret back door. The 'crimes' she chooses to probe into are prevalently of a petty, mean or coarse sort, at once cause and effect of malaise in the social microcosm. And in the light of the few but pointed references to religious practice occurring in the novel, for example to Sunday observance at Kirk or RC chapel – the latter, it is emphasized, attended also by the tinker-women – it is tempting to define the distinctive traits of its characters in terms of the time-honoured catalogue of the Seven Deadly Sins.[12]

Among these, predictably, Lust gains most prominence in all quarters, whether as personally pursued and relished or as the object of obsessive gloating curiosity. Among the incomers it marks Billy, with his proclivity to look elsewhere for what he cannot immediately obtain from his wife, and also Christa's compulsive fascination with Adam (who also embodies the masculine insouciance and the virtually unfeeling sexuality of the tinker outsiders). Among the residents, Dolina's careless promiscuity stands out in contrast with the clandestine love of Jean and Calum – an affair that actually everybody in Finavay knows and gossips about, and which is the man's refuge from his bleak ruin of a marriage.

All the other deadly sins have some part in connoting the atmosphere and determining the events in the novel: Greed dominates Calum's wife Nora, who filches her husband's money in revenge for his betrayal and as a nest-egg for her future, driving him in turn to trade on Dolina's crass sensuality as a way of recovering his losses. More widespread, in the cheap form of assuming one's moral superiority and right to condemn one's neighbour deprivation, is Pride, the source of all the scandal delightedly exchanged by the prim women shopping at the butcher's. Compared to this debased Pride, other vices - like Gluttony in the predictable Scotch form of drunkenness, and Sloth - leave the impression of being just slightly reprehensible failings: habitual in Billy, and at least occasional in young Finlay. More than wilful self-indulgence they appear to be a reaction to, or an escape from, frustrations undergone at the hands of women. A like extenuation could be made for the sin of Wrath, seeing that the causes of the guilt and despair flaring out in Calum's outbursts of violence on two occasions are women of such diverse, or rather antithetical tempers, as Nora and Dolina.

The most disturbing impact, however, is made by the last Deadly Sin, Envy: its tainted spirit, breathing in the background of this social microcosm, casts a deeper cloud on its atmosphere than the malicious envy of the 'bodies' on the community of Barbie. In Douglas Brown's novel, Envy was indeed a widespread sentiment with all people aiding and abetting each other in it, but it was also conducted partly out of revenge for the taunts received from their proud victim. In *Speak, Adam* however Envy is found in a concentrated, quintessential state, like a liquor distilled in the veins of an individual who refuses to accept the fact that goods are unequally distributed in this world. Envy rages at the happiness or well-being of people to whom no offence can be imputed, save that of being luckier than oneself in worldly gifts, and longs to see those people deprived and disgraced, no other good being reaped by this save that of rejoicing in their loss.

Burgess' original strategy of contrast between small-town atmosphere and culture and those of the city consists in opposing this type of person, whom a radical resentment makes the natural antagonist to all that is free and broad-minded, to the world-wise Glaswegian, Billy. He very soon begins to perceive the malevolence of the person that his wife, faithful to her childhood memories of Finavay, believes sympathetic and trustworthy. Billy is not admitted to the feminine spelling-glass game, whose crude suggestions and revelations leave the reader at a loss to decide if the forces at play are mediumistic or merely psychological. Billy therefore cannot guess what cruel facts have warped that personality; but his insight, though incomplete, makes him distrust, and as a result the attempt to make him despise and reject his wife is defeated, and even encourages him further in the decision to stand by her and stay on in Finavay, in spite of the unfriendly atmosphere.

The sanity of Billy's 'live and let live' attitude, however, would not be sufficient to bring about the happy end we mentioned at the beginning of this introduction. Up until the penultimate sentence in the novel, malice seems destined to prevail, not only in the petty form of scandal but in the more venomous one of slander. And then, with the last half dozen lines, Burgess shocks the readers out of their disappointment at the ineffectualness of the *denouement* occurred in the previous chapter, by presenting them with one of the residents – and that one 'a pillar of the church'[13] – who, instead of sweeping the dirt under the carpet along with his neighbours, is about to confess to his own share of it. This character succeeds in breaking out of the stereotype of the hypocritical 'Presbyterian elder', and the only explanation suggested for the fact is that in his man-to-man encounter with *l'homme moyen sensuel*, or Billy, he has experienced genuine respect, understanding and solidarity, instead of the scathing reproach or the dismissive scorn that, in the depth of his shame, he dreaded.

Another refreshing aspect of this novel is that towards the end the readers' sympathies are made to shift from the characters and predicaments of females to those of males, in breezy disregard of what the mid-eighties tended to prescribe, at least to women authors. Though Christa's one direct exchange with the tinker matriarch Teresa shows both at their best, most open and sane, what finally proves even more interesting, surprising and attractive are Billy's unexpected power for comprehension, and the equally unforeseen but quite convincing change of heart manifested by Calum's decision to defeat slander with confession.

This resolve is presented with deft economy in the open ending. Calum's simple gesture and few words are the prelude to a disclosure that, however, is left suspended and unspoken for every reader to imagine freely, along with whatever reactions or consequences may follow. One thing however is certain, that the comic or bitter vignette of the small marginal community is replaced by the picture of a little world of fallible human beings, some of them at least subject to change, not all of them incapable nor unperceptive of the grace of friendliness.

In George Mackay Brown's *Hawkfall*,[14] there also exists in the title story a similar final twist as the last sentence subverts the process of decline into dreary conformity and sterility and opts instead for life and freedom. Although *Hawkfall* was written and published some years before *Speak, Adam*, Mackay Brown was not insensible to the fact that other writers were capable of a similar effective mirroring of human communities. As I recall, it was this master in the art of truthfully depicting village and small town life who recommended, when I visited him in the Spring of 1988, that I read Moira Burgess' novel. A recommendation carrying no mean distinction.

Valentina Poggi
Bologna, Italy

[1] See, Ian Campbell, (1981) *Kailyard*. Edinburgh: The Ramsay Head Press. pp. 97-98.

[2] Burgess, Moira, *The Glasgow Novel*. 3rd edition. Scottish Library Association and Glasgow City Council, 1999.

[3] Burgess, Moira, (1985) *Streets of Stone*, Edinburgh: The Salamander Press, and, (1987) *The Other Voice*, Edinburgh: Polygon.

[4] Burgess, Moira, (2008) *Mitchison's Ghosts: Supernatural Elements in the Scottish Fiction of Naomi Mitchison*. Glasgow: Humming Earth.

[5] Publication to be confirmed.

[6] See Barrie, J.M, (1889) *A Window in Thrums*.

[7] See MacLaren, Ian, (1894 rpt., 2007) *Beside the Bonnie Briar Bush*. Glasgow: Kennedy and Boyd.

[8] See Brown, George Douglas, (1901) *The House with the Green Shutters*.

[9] See Gibbon, Lewis Grassic, (1932) *Sunset Song*.

[10] See Shepherd, Nan, (1930) *The Weatherhouse* and (1928) *Quarry Wood*.

[11] See Kesson, Jessie, (1963) *Glitter of Mica* and (1983) *Another Time, Another Place*.

[12] The 'Seven Deadly Sins' also known as 'capital vices' or 'cardinal sins' were first identified by St. John Cassian (360-435 AD) and were refined by Pope Gregory the Great (540-604 AD). The identified sins are Pride, Wrath, Envy, Lust, Gluttony, Avarice and Sloth.

[13] Burgess, Moira, (1987 rpt., 2009) *Speak, Adam*. Glasgow: Kennedy and Boyd, p.9.

[14] Brown, George Mackay, (1974) *Hawkfall*.

1

Christa was sitting on the front steps in the sun; forgetting for one luxurious moment that she was the lady of the house, she had kicked off her shoes in abandon. North and east, over the sparkling harbour, the hills were gently blue. Below lay the town, shimmering in the summer air, deep in a Sunday morning sleep. The gaunt big house of Glenrosa was racked in under the hill so that the back rooms never got any sun, but it stood high over Finavay Bay, and on long-ago June days even Aunt Sarah had been known to sit out here. In a camp-chair, of course.

She stretched and flexed her bare toes on the old silky sandstone. 'Chrissie, child, haven't you got any *stockings* on?' Aunt Sarah would certainly have said. Christa put her head back, propped by the peeling doorpost, and closed her eyes against the warmly fingering sun.

Behind her eyelids a scarlet curtain flickered and drifted with the high light clouds. She heard two voices, a woman's and a man's, exchanging words in a fast, incomprehensible, familiar tongue. The breeze grew stronger against her upturned face, and carried with it a curious smell that nevertheless she knew. She pressed close to Aunt Sarah's neat tweed side, frightened, but why? Raucous and rich-smelling and unrespectable, something was passing by that was larger than life, wider than the little grey town. *Turn away, Chrissie —*

'Are you sleeping, Mrs Beresford?' said Ellen Macleod above her, almost on a laugh.

Christa opened her eyes with a start. In her dazzled view there were great vague figures on the road beyond the gate. 'Oh, Ellen, who is it?' she said in ridiculous fear.

'The tinks are back,' said Ellen, patient as ever, waiting to set down the tray of coffee-cups. 'That's all.'

'I'd forgotten —'

But they were exactly the same as they ever had been. An old tinker woman walked ahead, in a coneyskin coat with its lining hanging out, the stitching split open at one shoulder, the fur rubbed in patches to the bare skin. Her grey hair hung in hanks and her tweed skirt dipped up and down at the hem. Behind her slouched a tall red-headed man in a torn battledress jacket and greasy old trousers, and two paces behind him again came his woman, heavy-laden on this warm day with her long coat and fleecy boots. She had the high tinker cheekbones and the weather-reddened skin, and red-gold tinker hair straggled from under her woollen scarf. Strangeness hung about them as it had long ago in the sunny street when the high-piled carts of snottery yelling children passed, with the wailing of the pipes, the richly mingled smells. *Chrissie, that's the tinks, they're dirty, come away —*

'God's blessin' on ye, missis,' said the old woman in the rapid tinker way. The dark diamond eyes in her hard-worn brown face scanned Christa, placing and evaluating her, coldly proud. The young woman's coat flapped from one button: she was hugely pregnant, well into her last month. *Turn away, Chrissie, they've no sense of shame —*

The red-haired man was favouring Christa with a long, amused, unmistakable look; though she couldn't possibly have seen, the old woman turned on the man and raked him with a rattle of the tinker cant, their own private language, harsh and strange. Christa hastily pulled her skirt over her knees. The old woman jerked round and marched off down the road; she hadn't the slightest doubt that he would follow. The girl waddled after them, leaning back to accommodate her swollen load.

'I wonder what that was all about,' said Ellen, cool and composed.

Christa began to say, 'Didn't you see — ?' She could feel

the too-ready colour in her face. *They've no sense of decency, Chrissie, they're dirty, come away* —

Billy came out of the house and folded himself up on the steps beside her. His right hand, a cigarette between two fingers, drummed a casual husbandly tattoo up and down her spine. She felt her jaw ache as she forced a smile.

'You might have brought the table over for Ellen,' she reproached him. She jumped up, away from the hand that had flattened to smooth over her shoulder-blade, and made to fetch it herself, though to her annoyance Billy's long arm hooked it over before she got there. The beastly little table had been rickety even in Aunt Sarah's time: its curlicues dated back long before Glenrosa's boarding-house days. It rocked dangerously under the coffee tray.

'I think there might be a wing nut missing, Mr Beresford,' Ellen said. 'We would be as well to check it before they come.'

'Oh, I'll do that, Mrs Macleod,' said Billy charmingly. 'It won't take a minute.'

'There's time yet and plenty of it,' said Ellen. Slow attractive highland voice, slow smile that lit up her high-boned face with its thoughtful dark eyes: oh, Ellen's going to be good for me, Christa thought. She's just what I need, somebody my own age who knows the ins and outs of the town. I would rush at the job, and that's not how things are done in Finavay. She sat down again and reached out for the cup of coffee Ellen had poured.

'Oh, Mrs Beresford, what would you like Dolina to be at while you're out?'

Christa considered. 'Has she done all the bedrooms?'

'We did them first, Mrs Beresford. Do you remember they were badly needing aired?'

'Oh yes. Well, I know, Ellen, could you both work, on the kitchen today? I thought I'd do a blitz on the baking this week and get the freezer stocked up.'

'I'll go and find her then. I left her counting your teaspoons,' said Ellen, 'but it has maybe proved too much for her.'

'Finlay went round the side of the house a minute ago,' said Billy, amused. 'Maybe he's proved too much for her.'

And on the word his hand, complete with cigarette, slipped up to rest on the back of Christa's neck.

'Billy, you'll set fire to my *hair*.' Christa pushed the hand away with a sound that wasn't entirely a laugh. 'Ellen,' she said, 'I've been meaning to ask you —'

She paused and looked around.

'They'll hardly catch what you say from up here,' said Ellen with a twitch of her mouth.

Christa did laugh this time, because indeed there wasn't a soul to be seen. All the souls were attending to their saving, the Protestants down in the square and the Catholics up on the hill; you could see the whole town from Glenrosa where it stood high on the chapel road. But Ellen had taken some trouble to warn her about careless talk. 'I would watch it, Mrs Beresford, walls have ears. You maybe wouldn't notice when you'd be here staying with your auntie, but they're terrible gossips, the Finavay folk.' Christa couldn't say whether she'd noticed or not; in her memory it was always summer in Finavay, always holiday-time, visitors scattered to the hills and the shore, grown-ups at work, and in the quiet sunny streets hardly anyone about.

Except the tinks . . .

Still, she didn't intend to get things wrong at the start. As she nodded back towards the open front door she found herself whispering, the landlady's small niece again whom the visitors weren't supposed to see. 'No, I wondered about Dolina, that's all. Is she the kind of girl who – you know – that we would have to watch, I mean in that way?'

Ellen looked shocked.

'Only I know –' Again the quick colour ran up under her

skin. Oh come on, you aren't ten years old now . . . ' – she hasn't any family in the town, and I wouldn't want her to – well –'

Billy was grinding out his cigarette in the saucer as if his life depended on extinguishing the last spark.

'I don't believe your aunt had any worries with her,' said Ellen rather carefully.

'Your aunt wouldn't have noticed,' observed Billy, 'if she'd done it on the dining-room table.'

This time it was Ellen's face which went red; no wonder, Christa thought in total horror. She heard Ellen say sternly, 'She's precocious right enough, is Dolina. And her mother before her, which was why she left the town.' Ellen seemed to pause, looking without expression at Billy's shirt open to his navel and the yard of bare leg below Christa's skirt, but all she went on to say was, 'Dolina once told my Mairi that she wanted to run a brothel when she grew up. Luckily Mairi understood it to be a kind of soup-kitchen.'

Christa instantly regretted her nervous giggle. Billy grinned and flicked the shreds of the mangled cigarette off his long fingers. 'The question is,' he said, leaning forward in an interested way, 'what did Dolina understand it to be?'

'I'll go and start on the kitchen then,' Ellen said. She walked into the house with her head held high.

Billy reached for the cigarettes, cocking an eye at Christa like a naughty boy. 'I think you embarrassed Ellen there,' she said. It wasn't quite as much as she wanted to say.

'If she was really embarrassed,' said Billy, 'she'd have gone away directly after the dining-table.'

He got up and stretched, smiling smugly down at her, his fair hair falling over his dark-lashed blue eyes that sometimes, thought Christa in vexation, saw more than you were ready for. He didn't bear a grudge. 'See you at the steamer and we'll meet Robin Redbreast together?'

'*Linnet,*' said Christa, reaching up to whack him. 'Sure you won't join us? Won't be time for picnics once they come.'

'No, no,' said Billy. 'Last year's Wimbledon highlights.'

'But you watched every ball last year.'

'I know,' said Billy, and went whistling in.

Christa leaned back against the warm doorpost; behind her, through an open window, the Wimbledon highlights began to murmur and ping. In the sunny little town below, the grey kirk slept in its silent square lined with farmers' cars: no sign of life yet around its heavy dark doors. Fishing boats danced at the quay in the glittering water, though not nearly so many as once there had been. She'd filled a notebook one summer with their names, *Felicia, Dileas, Stella Maris, Mairead B.* 'Chrissie Forrest, where have you *been?* That's your lunch ruined. And is that tar you've got on your shoes?' Aunt Sarah said.

Above on the headland the red sandstone Catholic church lifted its strong gable over the calm waters of Finavay Bay and the tide-rips outside. Must go up there, she lazily thought. Fresh air, sea breezes, wasn't that why we came to Finavay? Well, partly why . . . Yes, we'll walk up there. Up behind the church, where the cliff drops away: nothing up there but blue sky, the world curving round.

Oh, it's all still here. I was right to come, she thought. Out of all the trouble and mess; we've left that behind. The boarding-house bit, no problem, I can cope. She breathed gently, lapped in the soft sweet air. Nothing bad can happen here. We'll fit in. And Billy likes it too, so he'll behave.

'Dolina has something to show you,' Ellen said from the door.

Out on the road now, as Christa blinked, were ordinary people, children, grannies, family groups, a decorous Sunday promenade. 'Oh, Ellen, that's surely not the church coming out? I'm supposed to be meeting Jean.'

'I think it will be the Roman Catholics. They finish a bit before the kirk.'

'I thought for a minute,' said Christa, half-laughing, 'the tinkers were coming down from the chapel.'

'Maybe they were,' said Ellen, raising her eyebrows. 'I believe some of them will be RCs right enough.'

'But they don't – surely they don't –' Christa aged ten, bored in the hard dark-wood pew under the soft overwhelming camphor-scented shade of her aunt's good fur coat. *Everybody goes to church, Chrissie . . .* She sucked, not crunched, the one permitted peppermint, staring through the plain high window at the vault of sky above the sunny town. What if the black oak doors had burst open, and in had swung the tinks, bright-eyed, rank-smelling, frighteningly without shame? The imperious old woman and the swollen girl, and, looking around hot and eager, the greasy-breeked red-haired man. What if they had? How would it be?

'Oh, I don't know what they *do*,' said Ellen ominously, 'but they go, and I suppose they will be made welcome. The Catholics are funny that way. Everybody in Finavay goes to church. I noticed that very strong when I came down from the glen.'

'I shouldn't have asked you to work on a Sunday, Ellen.'

'No, no,' said Ellen, for some reason a little distant, 'you were needing the help. Anyway I wasn't wanting to go today. It's a new minister.'

'Isn't he as good as the old one?'

'I couldn't be saying, Mrs Beresford.' That seemed to deal with the minister. 'It's this thing Dolina found among the spoons. Where are you away to now, you silly lassie?'

There was a giggle and a scuffle behind her in the hall, but Dolina emerged demure and alone. She was really the picture of a perfect Highland maidservant, round rosy face, dark curly hair, healthy figure slightly straining at the buttons of her pink nylon overall. Silently she held out a small jeweller's box, which Christa opened with matching gravity. It contained a silver napkin-ring, brassy from neglect. Christa rubbed at the tarnish and tilted the ring to the light.

'Aunt Sarah's,' she said, 'or Granny's, I suppose. This house is full of things I don't know about. As a matter of fact it's been such a rush since we came, I haven't even found the back door yet.' She almost thought she saw the beginning of a smile on the little Dutch-doll face, but Dolina wasn't sure enough of her new boss. 'Would you like to put it on the dresser, Dolina, and I'll clean it up when I have time?'

Dolina disappeared as silently as she had come, and Christa grinned at Ellen Macleod. 'Better go with her,' she said, 'in case Finlay proves too much for her again.'

Ellen looked a little surprised. 'Oh, Finlay's away,' she said. 'I couldn't be having him under my feet and work to be done. I'm after chasing him out the side gate ten minutes ago.'

Christa was cold in the sun. No, don't start, she thought. Don't start again. Her teeth were clenched: that wasn't another giggle? Last year's Wimbledon highlights boomed from the open window, and she looked directly into Ellen's dark eyes.

Ellen said, 'I see the church doors are open, Mrs Beresford. Can you spot Nurse Lambert yet? There's Calum Macnair on the step.'

Christa's mouth uttered something not at all directed by her mind, and Ellen said, 'Yes, that's right, do you remember he's in the main street? Your auntie spoke well of his meat, though mind you he's not cheap.'

Christa's eyes cleared: she was looking down the long street again, but now there were figures in the townscape, clustered on the steps of the round grey-steepled church. I don't care, she thought. I really don't care. We got through it before. It can't be that bad again.

The minister came out, grasping his black gown on his shoulders as it rose in the sea breeze like the wings of a settling bird. Dark-suited men, tweed-suited ladies in hats, and the portly figure of Calum Macnair the butcher, standing one step down from the minister, inclining his heavy head in greeting here and there. 'I suppose he's an elder,' she said.

'Oh, he's a pillar of the church is Calum.'

'Well,' said Christa, taking a breath, 'it won't fall down in a hurry.'

She looked again straight at Ellen, daring her to show pity, daring her even to admit that something hung unsaid. Ellen's level mouth lifted at the corners; almost you might have called it a smile.

'I've never seen a thin butcher,' she said.

'Oh, Ellen, you're a tower of strength,' said Christa, suddenly warm with gratitude, liking, nearly love. 'How could I run this place without you?'

2

And she'll make a bourach of the business, Ellen thought.

She narrowed her eyes and stared coldly at Christa, who was diving around the steps looking for her shoes, her dark-red hair coming loose as usual, lifting in the June breeze like seaweed in the ebb. Her heart's not in it, Ellen thought. She should be down on her knees with a scrubbing-brush, not sitting on her backside drinking coffee that somebody else has made. She'll bugger it up inside a year. And if she doesn't, he'll drink the profits. 'I'll just take those things indoors,' she said with a pleasant smile.

The silly table jiggled worse than before, and Christa's long eyelashes flickered in one of her little-girl glances; acting it as usual, since she'd never see thirty again. 'He will fix it,' she offered apologetically as Ellen steadied the tray.

Any half-handy man would have done it in the same movement that he picked the table up, but not that layabout, thought Ellen. And Madam's not caring, as long as he's there and a man. 'While he has the tools out,' she said, 'if he has a moment, could he glance at the window in the east bedroom? It'll neither stay open nor closed.'

'Damp, that's the trouble,' said Christa with a confident air.

Oh, you would need your domestic science diploma for that one, Ellen thought; considering the bedrooms were shut up for eight months and blue-mouldy when we opened the doors. 'Yes, that'll be it, Mrs Beresford,' she said.

Christa slipped on her shoes and stood up. 'I'd better go. Jean will be waiting. I'll ask him about the window — ' she called back over her shoulder, already halfway to the gate.

When you're finished stravaiging around the countryside, that's to say. Ellen stood with a stone face for a moment, watching Christa run down the road. You could see the whole town from Glenrosa, and though Christa didn't know it yet, by God could the town see you. Oh wait you, thought Ellen, straight-backed on the doorstep of Glenrosa; oh I hope I'm there to see, my lassie, when you take on Finavay town.

She turned to go into the house, but she didn't need to go far; through the open window she could see Billy on the sofa, and she could see Dolina perched on the arm of a chair beside him, and Billy's hand was where it shouldn't have been. Ah, they're all the same, said Ellen's thoughts from a cold distance; and the wicked thrill possessed her, body and soul.

Oh it wasn't right, the two of them, lolling about half-dressed, cuddling on the doorstep, old enough to know better; loose talk, loose behaviour, and a silly wee lassie like Dolina taking it all in. 'Where are you, Dolina?' she snapped, stalking indoors.

Dolina in a panic shot out into the hall, slightly disarranged. No sound from the room, except the television's drone; easy enough to picture him, though, spreadeagled on the sofa, maybe smiling a bit, quite pleased with his carry-on. You could tell by looking at him that he was like the rest of them. He didn't care.

3

Oh, Billy, thought Christa, flying down the road; oh hell, what does it matter, a tickle in the hall? She paused to catch her breath as she reached the square. I should have kissed him goodbye, though. He'll think — he'll feel — no, I don't care. It will all work out. It's a new life here. We're starting again.

She moved awkwardly into the square under the gaze of the ladies on the church steps. Madly she wondered whether she would recognize Jean. If the tinkers hadn't changed in twenty-five years, neither had the ladies: all those good suits, all those hats. *Everybody goes to church, Chrissie* ... Perhaps I'll go next Sunday, she thought. Or I'll never fit in.

Calum Macnair turned with a kind of lumbering courtesy, wondering no doubt who she was and what she was at. She had a laughable split-second picture of the pink and breathless girl he must see, pushing her untidy red hair away from her face —

She blinked in amazement as his little hot brown eyes fixed greedily on hers.

No, no, Christa. Just because you're a little worked up about Billy, what a state to be in! Calum Macnair said civilly, 'Oh, Mrs Beresford, is it Nurse Lambert you'll be looking for?' and he was a sober-suited fat middle-aged man, an elder of the kirk. 'She stayed behind to see about the flowers. There she's thonder, look, having a word with Mrs Macnair.'

It was hard to see Mrs Macnair, a wispy little creature deep in the shadow of the porch, but there was no mistaking Jean beside her, plump and confident and talking enough for three. 'Oh, Christa, there you are! The car's over at the no-parking sign. Listen, I hope you don't mind, I said I'd give them a run up to the site. We can go further on for our picnic, it's lovely up the hill —'

'Site?' said Christa, catching a passing word as it flew.

'The tinkers' camp, you know. You'll remember the travellers, surely? They used to be always round the door at Glenrosa, though it wasn't your aunt who encouraged them. I think Bella was a soft mark, and there would always be the broth-pot on the hob.'

'I don't really remember. I was pretty young, of course.' *Feech, Chrissie, the tinks, come away, turn away —*

'They're up in the birchwood again. I hope they keep it decent this time, they're kind of careless whiles. I've got this wee traveller baby coming out of the cottage hospital, it's just him and his mother, they'll sit in the back —'

'How old?' said Christa sharply.

'Who?' said Jean in surprise. 'The wee one? Oh, he's a toddler really, two I'd think, just turned two.'

It's still too young. Too young to be safe. Oh, but the world has plenty of baby boys for me to see. 'Yes, all right, Jean,' she said.

'You'd probably see them about the town, though, when you'd be at the shops with your auntie,' said Jean, driving neatly through the last of the churchgoers in the square.

Calum Macnair paused on the steps to let them pass, fastening the buttons of his smooth black coat. His thin little wife hovered behind him, a shadow in a shade. His small eyes rested on the car with no trace of expression. Oh God, I'll have to take a grip, thought Christa. I imagined the whole thing. Next Sunday I'll go to church. With a hat on.

'Macafee's their name. The travellers. They're the local tribe,' said Jean, oblivious at the wheel. She raised a hand in acknowledgement as they drove past a little knot of ladies in hats, who, unlike Calum, recognized the car with nods and smiles.

It was a heavy pad of muscle, not really fat at all, bulking out the shoulders of his Sunday coat.

Alicky Gillespie's plump widow Bethia said to her friend

Kate Frizell, the lawyer's spinster sister, 'She's a wild-looking sight for a Sunday. Who is she to her own name again?'

'Chrissie Forrest, I'm sure you know, Bethia. Did I not tell you Glenrosa was willed to her father?'

'And she's married on to a man Beresford. That's hardly a Finavay name.'

'No, no, he's a pure incomer, he has nobody in the town at all. Her skirt's far too short,' said thin Kate, glancing smugly downwards. 'Here though, did you see wee Jean Lambert speaking to Nora Macnair?'

'Oh, she has the cheek of the devil.'

'You'd never think it to look at her,' said Kate. 'And she isna exactly what you'd call braw.'

'Whiles I think they're the worst.'

'Well, it's you has the experience, Bethia,' Kate humbly allowed. Bethia looked less than pleased at that.

Calum Macnair gave a hand with closing the church doors, though it wasn't his job and he wheezed a bit as he tackled the heavy bolts. The beadle had disappeared: with any kind of work on hand he wasn't slack, the same Sandy, to find some important mission like dusting the pulpit Bible. 'Are you all right there, Mr Macnair?' asked young Mr Carrington, flashing teeth and glasses at the top of the steps.

'Och, fine altogether, meenister. Away you to your dinner before it's cold.'

The minister giggled nervously and off he went to his wife and child. After fifteen years of a bachelor in the manse the Guild ladies had gone crazy over this novelty: soft English fair hair and big blue eyes, and toys apologetically swept up off the parlour floor. 'It's more natural some way,' they one and all agreed.

Right enough, thought Calum sourly, closing the side door on the vision of the minister's flapping sports jacket and long colt's legs, hurrying home to something hot. A slack time before the evening service, now Sunday school had been moved to the morning, and the wee blond boy likely still taking an afternoon nap, what was to hinder the man? It's natural, ladies, said Calum savagely, picturing their horrified faces, and his own mouth twisted in a kind of sob.

Still, it was Sunday, so that wasn't so bad. Seven hours, maybe six and three quarters, to get through. Since there was nothing whatsoever left for him to do around the church, he rolled across the square to his battered little car. Nora was sitting there stifling with all the windows shut, her ratty fur collar turned up round her peaked white face. 'You managed to turn the door handle the day,' he remarked, squeezing in under the wheel. 'It's worth the effort, is it no'?'

'I still think you should lock it, Calum. It would be a terrible expense if it got stolen.'

'Ach, they're honest folk in Finavay,' he said, coaxing the ancient engine to life.

'But an incomer maybe, you canna be sure.'

'They wouldna need to be making a speedy getaway,' he said glumly. He stopped at the edge of the square to wave Bethia and Kate across, and the engine stalled of course. He worked on it impassively, feeling a pulse begin to beat in his head. Fat Bethia and skinny Kate swanned over the road, bowing. Bethia's Sunday dinners were namely in the town, even now that she only had young Finlay at home, and Kate always bought the very best cuts for the weekend, if it was the sausages and the corned beef in between times. 'I wonder you wouldna go to the Guild once in a while, Nora,' he said. 'There's Bethia Gillespie always pleasant to you.'

'Aye, to my face.'

You would sometimes think she wasna so daft. 'There'd be somebody you would get on with surely.' Guild meetings — who should know better than himself? — Tuesday nights, seven to nine. Just about long enough, if he was reckless and took the car. 'A friend you could talk to, that'd do you the world of good.'

'It's you would know about that,' she waspishly replied.

He drew a breath through his teeth, but fortunately she was away on another tack. 'How could I go to the Guild,' she girned, 'me that hasna a decent rag to wear?'

'Whose fault is that?' he shouted.

There didn't seem much left to talk about. 'Sandy Macrae's roses are coming on,' he desperately ventured as they drew up in the mean little street outside their peeling gate. Nora's glance at their own five moribund bushes was enough answer to that. It was even warmer inside the house than out. Nora turned on the weak gas-burner under the potatoes and listlessly prepared their Sunday dinner: as always, wet pink boiled ham, wilting lettuce, pebbly small tomatoes from the bottom of the box.

Calum grimly opened a can of beer, which was his Sunday treat, though Nora sighed and sniffed and mourned at the expense. His other Sunday treat. He checked his father's fob watch once again with the dusty parlour clock. Six and three quarter hours to go. Maybe six and a half.

4

Hughie Macafee didn't know his mother. Jean held out her arms to him, and the young nurses did their best with 'Who's got a wee smile for his mammy?' and 'Ah, he's just strange,' but Hughie only buried his pink face in Matron's smooth lilac bosom. He was blue-eyed and tow-headed like all those cheeky tinker children in the carts long ago. *Don't go near them, Chrissie, they're dirty* — His round cheeks shone like sealskin and his soft-washed hair curled round Matron's finger. The front hall of the cottage hospital fairly pulsed with professional cheer and encouragement, but at the back of her own tumbling thoughts Christa felt Jean's worry about this clean, shy little boy.

'You're not moving on just yet, are you, Mrs Macafee?' said Matron.

'No'till the berry-pickin', nurse,' said Hughie's mother with the harsh whining tinker tune. She was the very pregnant young woman Christa had seen on the chapel road. She stood humbly on the hospital steps in her loose coat and big boots, under the warm sun, showing no distress at Hughie's strangeness. On her brown, high-boned face there was not much expression at all. Mrs Macafee? thought Christa in a kind of surprise. That tink, Aunt Sarah would have said.

'Nurse Lambert is taking you home now and she'll look in to see how he's going on. But he's a picture of health, aren't you, Hughie?'

Hughie did not reply. Jean with unsuspected firmness lifted him out of Matron's arms and placed him in his mother's far from eager grasp. 'There you are, Veronica,' she said. 'He's doing fine now, and see the nice wee red jersey the girls knitted for him. You'll be wanting to get up the road.'

Hughie's plump baby body fitted securely into his mother's

hard arms. Christa felt it; and she felt, as if she held him indeed, his silky head cuddling into the angle of her neck and shoulder. I should have told Jean before now, she thought, and she wouldn't have brought me. Oh, I should have known, I shouldn't have come.

It was a long haul for Jean's little car up the glen road to the tinkers' wood under the green shoulder of Finavay Hill. Christa in the front seat was aware through every nerve and muscle of Veronica and Hughie silent in the back. She wasn't even talking to him. Surely you would talk to your little boy?

As they bucketed round a steep hairpin bend Christa looked back and saw Finavay cupped round its harbour, a matchstick-model town. The grey church in the square, no cars round it now, everybody sure of salvation for this week and home for Sunday dinner; the fishing boats at the quay, the jumbled houses at the quayhead. One of those little old houses was Ellen Macleod's, but Ellen was careful with information and hadn't yet revealed exactly which. The red church with its high uncompromising cross, up on the headland in the sun and wind; no mystery about Jean's neat cottage below it, half-way up the chapel road, where Christa had already been to tea. No secrets at all, thought Christa gratefully, about Jean.

On this side of the bay the glen road faced sweetly south, and the hazels and birches were in full leaf. Cool sparkling air washed in through the car windows. Christa got out at Jean's direction to open a gate, and the little car strained up over a rutted track between high green banks where the bracken was beginning to uncurl.

'You'll see a difference even since you arrived,' said Jean. 'The summer comes on suddenly when it does come.'

'It was all just beginning,' said Christa. Only ten days since they had been slowing down at Glenrosa's front gate, high above the rippled bay, under an infinite vault of blue spring sky. 'There's a cuckoo!' she had cried in delight. Billy, thoughtfully negotiating the rather tight turn, had said 'Unless it's coming down the road at sixty, I'll attend to it later.'

But he had grinned at her, out on the gravel driveway, as she searched her bag for the gaol-sized key. 'Just the way you remembered it?' She nodded, determined on bliss, though the flowerless shrubs were higher and darker than her childhood hideouts, and Aunt Sarah would have fainted at the state of the windows. They heaved open the front door, and the dank air of the long-closed house came out in a rush, tainted with damp and rot and hidden decay. After a moment: 'If I put my foot down we could be back in Glasgow tonight,' said Billy.

Jean glanced at Christa as they rattled over the dry summer mud. 'You've hardly had much chance to observe the wildlife,' she said. 'Somebody should have gone in and cleaned that house before you had to face it.'

'Well, I had the keys in Glasgow, I didn't think of asking —'

'It's a rambling one,' said Jean sternly. 'I'm not at all sure I didn't smell dry rot.' They pulled over a rise, and on the far side of the bay there was Glenrosa in its heavy nest of thick dull leaves. The sun had gone from the front doorstep long ago. Jean sighed. 'As long as it's going to be habitable for Saturday,' she said.

'We just had to tear into the front rooms and the bedrooms. This week we'll do the kitchen. It's been absolutely hectic. There's acres of attics and back corridors we haven't set foot in yet,' said Christa, 'and I don't suppose we'll have time now till September.' She wound down the window another six inches and closed her eyes to the kiss of the hill breeze. Damp and rot and decay, who cares? This is beautiful, she thought again. This is why we came.

'There's the cuckoo,' said Jean. 'It's late. Its voice will break any time now. Hughie, do you hear the cuckoo?'

Veronica in the back seat leaned forward suddenly to look out of the window, as if she expected to see the cuckoo. Indeed cuckoo calls were bubbling all round them, nearer and shriller than the first pure sound. 'Wingless cuckoos those,' said Jean, glancing at Christa again, inexplicably amused.

Screams of laughter burst like fireworks around the car, and on every side children sparked out of the bracken, dashing ahead down the track. The hog-back tents looked as if they had been there for ever, grey like winter grass, on level ground under a sheltering rocky bluff. Jean parked between an upended cart and an old van with its bonnet open at a rakish tilt. She got out and opened the door for Veronica, and Christa rather nervously got out too, in the nippy woodsmoke smell of a cooking stove, quivering the air with its rising heat.

Veronica in her heaviness was slow to struggle out of the awkward little car, but she wouldn't hand Hughie to Jean. By the time she was steady on her feet the bright-eyed children were pressing in, poking with sharp grimy fingers, giggling and hissing. From his mother's arms Hughie looked down at them with more than a tinge of doubt.

Veronica set him down on the trampled grass, gave him a pat on the bottom, and said, 'G'wan now, Hughie, away an' play yersel'.'

Instantly he clung to her, burying his face in her draggly skirt. The children shrieked in mocking joy. 'G'wan, ye wee bugger,' said Veronica, not particularly annoyed. Christa stepped forward half a pace.

'There's your granny, Hughie,' said Jean in her blessedly professional way.

Well, she could have been seventy, or fifty, or ninety, but she didn't look like anything so homely as a granny. She had appeared outside one of the tents, though you couldn't imagine her humbling herself to stoop through its low doorway. She addressed three words to the over-excited children and they scattered away as if Hughie had turned red-hot. She stood like an empress, drawing her big shawl about her head. That was her *best* fur coat this morning, thought Christa, and wanted to laugh. A sweep of the fierce old eyes put an end to that.

She gave no sign that she recognized Christa, but she nodded graciously to Jean.

'That was a good job ye done there, nurse,' she said. 'Gie the nurse a cigarette.'

She spoke into the air. Behind her a man ducked out of the tent and came forward with a bit of a swagger, as if to imply that he had been coming anyway. Of course he was the redheaded man from the road, and he recognized Christa all right. In the one well-judged moment when his back was squarely placed to the old woman, his long mouth drew back in a kind of smile. His broken front teeth were sharp like a cat's. He turned to Jean, seriously honouring her little plump figure in its good tweed suit, and held out a squashed cigarette packet.

'Oh, it was the hospital, not me,' said Jean. 'Another time you wouldn't let the wee fellow get so far through, would you? Thanks, I don't smoke.'

In totally normal courtesy, except perhaps for that insolent smile, the young man offered the packet to Christa.

'Thanks,' said Christa. She hadn't smoked since she was sixteen. She fumbled the cigarette to her mouth: Hughie's young father struck a match on the seat of his denims and held the light in his cupped hand while she inexpertly inhaled. She was aware that Jean was watching, not a little amazed. She felt as if the whole encampment was watching. Not for the first time, she wished she hadn't come.

'Je-*sus*,' said Hughie's father, shaking the match-flame out as it licked his palm. 'Have ye got it now?'

Christa looked up with watering eyes and he swam before

her, marigold hair brighter than Billy's, brilliant blue eyes narrowed, interested, amused. *Chrissie, turn away* — He wasn't at all like Billy. It wouldn't be at all the same.

'That'll dae!' said the old woman sharply. Christa jumped like a guilty child. The red-headed man, blank-faced, obediently moved away.

Jean was saying to the grandmother with due respect, 'I might call in again, Mrs Macafee.'

'It'll no' be necessary, nurse.'

'Oh, not to see him,' said Jean briskly. 'Only the other wee ones in the ward were wanting to give him sweeties to say goodbye, and they didn't get them bought yesterday. It's just not to disappoint them, you know how wee ones are —'

Mrs Macafee indicated a nod. 'If that's a' it is then,' she said. She watched impassively as Jean ruffled Hughie's small blond bullet head. 'God bless ye, nurse,' she said. 'Open the car door for the nurse.' It was another directive to Hughie's father, as promptly obeyed.

Christa, her cheeks hot, got in by herself at the other side. Next Sunday, she thought ridiculously, I'll go to church. With a hat on. Sucking peppermints. What if the door bursts open and the tinks march in? She felt the nervous giggle rising again in her throat. Oh, how would it be?

Jean adjusted her seat-belt and paused, squinting up through the window. 'Clinic on Tuesday, Veronica?'

'Aye, well, I might,' said Veronica, with an involuntary flicker of the eyes back towards the tents.

Jean sighed. 'Don't rush the wee fellow anyway, will you? It's been a long time.'

'Ah, would we dae that, nurse? God's blessin' on ye, nurse,' said his grandmother earnestly. Hughie in an access of strangeness butted his head up under Veronica's skirt. 'Gerrowa that, ye dirty wee cunt,' said his father in some amusement; which was the first time, Christa realized with a twist of her stomach, that he had paid any attention at all to his little boy.

Fiercely she jammed her half-smoked cigarette into Jean's virgin ashtray. Jean did not comment, which was a mercy. That very silly episode was over, the impulse of interest gone as suddenly as it had come. And why had it ever come? Her fingers now were rank with stale cigarette smoke. When she bent her head to the shielded match-flame, she had breathed in a different smell.

'Whit happened tae his blanket?' said a hoarse loud voice in her ear. The old woman's face loomed in through the open window: the smoky breath of the campfire hung about her greasy snake-locked grey hair. She continued winningly, as if she hadn't noticed Christa recoil: 'D'ye no' mind his bonnie wee blanket, nurse? I wrapped it aboot him wi' ma ain hands the night ye took him away.'

'I'll see to it, Mrs Macafee,' said Jean with great good humour. The little car turned and jounced down the track. Jean blew out her cheeks and said 'If you'd seen the rag it was ... Never mind. Makes another excuse to go back. Veronica's not the worst as mums go, but she doesn't get to blow her nose without asking Theresa.'

Christa said in alarm, 'They won't – will they be good to him?' She craned over her shoulder to look back at the camp. The children had come out of the bracken again, but among their tangled saffron mops Hughie's downy head was not to be seen. She thought she could hear him crying, pressed against his sluttish uncaring mother, lost and forlorn. She was close to crying herself. 'They never even spoke to him!' she said.

'Oh, now we've gone they'll speak all right,' said Jean absently. She turned the car on to another half-forgotten track that faded into the heather a few yards up the hill. 'I just wish I knew what they'll be saying.'

But up in the bracken high above the bay, with egg and cress sandwiches and a flask of coffee, Jean was more cheerful. 'They're very good to children, in their way,' she said. 'Only he's been in hospital so long.' Rather fiercely she turned her plump worried face to Christa. 'I had to take him in. Middle of January and snow on the ground, and this wee soul in a tent, burning up with pneumonia. We got him in time and he'd have been out before you knew it. Only just after he went in, they struck camp and disappeared.'

There they go, thank the Lord . . . There they come again . . . Chrissie, run and tell Maggie to shut up the hens . . . 'Well, they do come and go, don't they?' said Christa cautiously.

'Not so much in the winter. But there was trouble,' said Jean, and hesitated over her words. 'There was a rumour of trouble. And they only came back last week. So nobody quite knew what to do with him, and he's been away from them nearly six months. That matters to the tinks. He's different now, you see.'

'He's clean,' said Christa lightly. If she kept things pretty light, she thought, she could cope with Hughie Macafee.

'Tinkers aren't dirty,' said Jean with unexpected sharpness. 'For heaven's sake, would they survive? It's not a dirty smell that's off them. But now Hughie smells like us. Different.'

She sat nibbling her thumbnail, looking down over the greening hill to the silken sweep of Finavay Bay. Oh, leave it, Jean, cried Christa silently, while I can still cope. Very hard to cope with, the baby smell of Hughie's round pink cheeks.

'Ah well,' said Jean at last, 'what with the sweeties and the blanket, I'll be able to go back. I'll keep an eye on Theresa. As long as she doesn't take a spite to him, the rest will toe the line. She even keeps that son of hers in order most of the time. It's a blessing somebody can. He's a heller that one.'

'He's a right tink,' said Christa. Keep it light, keep it light . . . 'As Aunt Sarah would say.'

'I'll tell you something, Christa,' said Jean. 'He would be a heller supposing he was a — a —'

'An elder of the kirk?'

'A shopkeeper,' Jean said at the same moment. Her quick high embarrassed laugh seemed to come from somebody else. 'Mercy, there's the steamer!'

'Oh Lord, and I'm supposed to be meeting Linnet.' They bundled up the picnic in guilty haste.

'And that's you,' Jean panted over the boot-lid, 'your staff and all, in time for — '

'Saturday. Oh God, I've everything to do.' Christa slid into her seat. No time for picnics after this. Good. No time for dangerous people like Hughie Macafee. Or his father, the heller, the tink . . . 'I'll have to see Calum Macnair tomorrow about running an account.' And Jean didn't need to know by what odd connection the butcher had come to mind.

'He'll not be surprised to see you exactly,' said Jean, head bent over the catch of her seat-belt. 'Your auntie dealt with him all her days. He'd know you when you were a wee girl.'

From up on the hill the town had seemed a toy that you could hold in your hand. It was coming nearer as they juddered down the track, real houses now, Sunday-silent, curtained, closed. Behind the curtains life-size people, who knew Christa Beresford but whom Christa didn't know. They were at home. She was outside. 'I suppose —' she said, '— you wouldn't have a minute to come in with me tomorrow? He certainly knows you.'

'What makes you think that?'

Christa was taken aback. 'Well, you're the nurse,' she said, 'everybody knows you.'

The little car turned with care on to the main road. 'Monday's a bit busy for me,' said Jean. 'I'll have to check my diary.'

'I'll phone you, shall I?'

'Yes, well, don't phone tonight, though. I won't be in.'

'You mean there's somewhere to go on a Sunday in Finavay?'

Jean put down her sun-visor as the blue bay broke up in dazzling points of light. 'We'll have to step on it,' she said. 'It's amazing how quickly she makes in to the quay.'

5

Christa stopped at the front door to do her lady of the manor bit. 'How far? Gosh, that's only a step,' Linnet had said blithely on the phone. 'Don't think of bringing the car. One small bag, that's me.' Billy took the opportunity to put down the one small bag and flex his fingers. 'What the hell have you *got* in there?' he enquired.

The mistress of the house shot him one of her chillier looks, but Linnet only laughed, shaking the long fine light-brown hair out of her eyes. 'Oh dear, is it heavy?' she said. 'It's full of books, you see.'

'No clothes?' said Billy.

'An extra pair of jeans and lots of clean knickers,' said Linnet, earnest and wide-eyed. Billy could see that Christa dearly wanted to pack either Linnet or himself back off to Glasgow by the first available boat. Perhaps she couldn't decide which she could best spare.

But they were standing before the incredible pile that was Glenrosa, and Linnet won favour by gazing enraptured, hands clasped, at the turrets and crowsteps, the oriel windows, the barley-sugar drainpipes. When she was at last persuaded indoors and rummaging for comb and toothpaste in her little room up the back stairs, Billy leaned against the kitchen dresser and examined his galled palms. 'You might have let me whistle up that boy,' he said mildly. 'That's why they meet the steamer. They probably put it on their tax return.'

He should have remembered that Christa was touchy about tinkers. 'We'd never have seen him again,' she said with an irritated smile. She came over, all the same, and looked crossly at his hands. 'She must know perfectly well it's heavy,' she said.

'I think not,' said Billy. 'There'll always be some poor idiot who just happens to be going her way.'

'Well, she'll have to tie that hair back or it will go in the soup,' said Christa grimly as the light foot of her employee was heard on the attic stair.

Billy found it quite refreshing to see Glenrosa through Linnet's eyes. Christa had totally lost her sense of proportion about the place; of course she couldn't let herself be seen to have acquired a pig in a poke, and so the vast strange house had taken on the ambience of a stately home. As soon as she crossed the threshold you could hear the jingle of chatelaine's keys. Linnet, slim and tall in her jeans and bushwhacker shirt, didn't seem unduly crushed.

She certainly said the right things, though. She loved her little camceiled room, the twin of Dolina's, tucked as they both were far back under the hill so that they never got any sun. She loved the residents' lounge and the dining-room with their spacious high views over Finavay Bay, displayed by Christa as if she had personally gathered together the water and called it the sea. Christa looked sideways at her as they toured the bedrooms, but she didn't comment on the wide-open windows, and indeed the smell of damp did seem to be fading at last. That's a relief, thought Billy with a reminiscent grin.

And Linnet loved the kitchen, of course, which raised her score considerably. 'Ellen and Dolina have worked hard on this,' allowed Christa, every inch the boss. She and Linnet poked about together, discussing the selection of ovens and the big scrubbed deal table and the cupboards where the baking-tins lived, while Billy settled his shoulders against a door and let his mind wander along a pleasant track, improbably set off by the thought of the smell of damp.

Christa opened the door he was leaning on with the most rudimentary of apologies, explaining to Linnet that this one led to the pantry and that one to the scullery. In fact there were seven or eight doors leading off the kitchen, which intrigued Linnet no end. 'I bet you hardly know what you've got back there,' she remarked, opening one at random and peering into darkness.

'Well, as a matter of fact —' said Billy, mimicking, and Christa gave him a glare. 'Well, as a matter of *fact*,' she said crossly, 'we haven't found all the keys yet.'

'I like it, I like it!' cried Linnet with her bubbling laugh. Christa visibly relaxed. Billy could see her trying on for size the role of a lovable eccentric, with a house so big she couldn't count the rooms. She smiled kindly at Linnet, as if, after all, Linnet might do.

They moved up into the owner's flat for what Christa evidently saw as a little business talk: 'Please stay, Billy,' she said with insufferable graciousness. Billy sat down and clasped his hands round his crossed knees, and nodded and smiled as required, while he delicately stripped his wife to his pleasure, starting with the hair-ribbon, ignoring her cries.

He had just reached an interesting stage when Linnet stood up to go: as he should have foreseen, any business talk involving Linnet was likely to be short indeed. Always the gentleman, he stood up too.

'No, no, I've taken up enough of your time,' she was exclaiming. Billy had missed a bit of the chat, for which Christa's lace-trimmed petticoat was entirely to blame, but he suspected that Christa might have offered escort services for a tour of the town. 'I'll leave you in peace, just the two of you.' Linnet beamed around the compact little flat, enthusiastic and innocent and with an outstanding talent for putting her foot in her mouth. 'No family yet, Mrs Beresford?' she cheerfully enquired.

Lacy petticoats, the spindrift on the sea: below, the blood and water, silent and dark. Billy waited for Christa to answer, but he didn't know what she would say. He willed her to say 'No, not yet.' Just that; then he would come in with some silly-bugger remark about something completely different, and the corner would be turned.

She wasn't going to say anything at all. After all those fruitless hours, sweat-slick body wrenched with its unresting, unwilling flux, when they had politely asked him to leave, she had been as silent, pale and dry-lipped, facing her mystery. Some fucking soap-opera had chattered on the box as he sat in the day-room among the visitors, knowing it was going wrong. He leaned his whole length against the door and put his head lazily back and said into the air, 'We had a stillborn baby earlier this year.'

Linnet's pretty, clever face went white. 'Oh, I'm really sorry,' she said. There were tears in her ridiculous earnest eyes.

'That's all right, Linnet,' said Billy, and gathered himself for the necessary silly-bugger remark; which he managed remarkably well.

As they stood some minutes later at the side door, waving Linnet off on her exploration of the town, he said tentatively, 'You didn't mind, did you?'

'Of course I minded,' said Christa tightly.

Well, somebody's got to say it some time. He bit that back. 'She'll never mention it again,' he said instead. 'I'm sure of that.' He put out his hand to push back a straggling curl from her sticky face, and she jerked her head irritably away. In a flash of anger himself, he ran through his scenario again from the hair-ribbon to the cries. It hadn't the same appeal. Christa looked bleakly back at him, and his heart turned over.

'So listen, love,' he said gently. Her face was bruised with held-back tears, woebegone as a schoolgirl's under the sweat-draggled hair; God, he thought, let's not mention schoolgirls, that's all it would take. 'We've got the house to ourselves, eh?'

'Oh, Billy, I don't know.'

'You didn't know this morning.'

'Well, it was a bit early.'

'What is it now, a bit late?'

'Look – ' she said, 'just let me bank up the Aga, would you?'

Strung up as he was, that made him laugh, and he caught her arms to share the joke. 'Last time we actually managed it,' he said, 'just as I got to the point of no return, you said, "Do you know, those bedrooms still smell of damp." '

She should have laughed with him, and laughing she was anybody's; but she turned away pettishly and made for the kitchen. 'Leave the bloody Aga alone!' he said between his teeth. He reached out to grab her; she deliberately struck off his hand and pushed against the kitchen door, which flew open and crashed against the wall.

'Who the hell are you?' said Billy, quite beyond himself with fury. There was a fat man standing, bowed and patient, in the middle of the kitchen floor.

But Christa laid a calming hand on his arm. She drew herself up, and he saw disbelievingly that she was pulling on, like a garment, her businesswoman's manner. She stood tall and in control, and with her own slim fingers put back the tendrils of damp hair from her hot angry face. 'It's the butcher,' she said. 'Do you want to see me, Mr Macnair?'

'Och, I wouldna want to be disturbing you, Mrs Beresford,' said the man. He slid a glance at Billy; evidently he could tell that the master was none too pleased. If he winks at me, thought Billy with unwonted savagery, I'll push his bloody face in.

But the butcher only stood there foursquare in his good Sunday coat, turning his black trilby round and round between his fat hands. The bulk of his heavy shoulders made him carry his head low: he looked up through his heavy brows like a humble bull. 'I thought you might be wanting to see me,' he said, 'about an account, you know.'

'But it's Sunday,' said Christa.

'The better the day,' said Mr Macnair, minting the phrase with delicate precision, 'the better the deed.'

For the next few minutes Billy could only watch in a kind of amazed despair. Christa introduced them properly. Calum Macnair presented his condolences to Billy over the death of Christa's aunt. 'Actually I never met the lady,' said Billy, but nobody took much notice, because suddenly the conversation turned to mince and sausages and stewing steak. Christa was at the peak of her performance as a landlady, thrifty and lucid and calm. It's a garment she puts on all right, thought Billy as he crossly went to the dresser and poured a generous dram for all three. It's a chastity belt.

Even Calum Macnair wouldn't insult a single malt with shop-talk, and he expanded his theme, nodding approvingly around the kitchen. 'You maybe wouldna believe this, Mrs Beresford, but I helped to build this very house.' Dutiful cries of incredulity from Christa. 'Anyway the extension, here at the back,' Calum Macnair admitted. 'I laboured to my uncle in the school holidays. He was a master mason, you know.' And you're a master crawler, you old sod, thought Billy with a charming smile. He hopelessly tried to catch Christa's eye. He wondered how it would be received if he were to lean forward and say 'Excuse me, Mr Macnair, but I'm rather anxious to go to bed with my wife.'

But the dram was lovingly drained and it was back to the mince, with footnotes on the flavour and freshness of local produce as against the false economy of bulk-buying from big suppliers. The only unanswered question, Billy silently remarked to the bottom of his glass, was whether the delivery man or Dolina had passed the word about Christa's new freezer, hardly forty-eight hours installed.

Ages later Calum put away his notebook and said 'Och, my gracious, that's never the time surely? Mrs Macnair will be thinking I'm away with the fairies.' Hell of a chance, thought Billy sourly. 'I'm sorry if I've disturbed your Sunday evening. I would sometimes be calling in on your auntie like this.' He handed his empty glass to Billy, who received it with a butler's deference, only in his imagination cracking it down across the slightly sweaty round bald head. The three of them moved in courteous leave-taking out of the kitchen, along the corridor, towards the side door. 'I suppose it's just the way we are in the Highlands. Neighbourly like. And here's me on my road home tonight, and I thought to myself, well, why not give Mrs Beresford a cry in?'

'How did you *get* in?' said Billy suddenly.

Calum Macnair paused, hat in hand, looking up at him in that powerfully humble way. 'I tried the front, but it was locked,' he said, 'so I just came in the back.'

'You did not,' said Billy, unreasonably set on putting the little bugger down. 'We were standing there.'

'No, the *back* door,' explained Calum Macnair most politely, and bowed himself away down the garden path.

'Now if you had let him go out the way he came in,' said Billy in the sudden silence, 'we might have found the bloody back door.'

'I must really look for it,' said Christa. She turned back towards the kitchen, and she was glowing as he hadn't seen her for weeks. Hell's teeth, thought Billy, perhaps I should grow a beer-belly and talk about mince.

'Get upstairs, woman,' he said, less than half in jest. She didn't even seem to hear. He saw that, still high on her efficiency kick, she actually intended to go and look for the back door there and then. He said, 'Not now, Christa, please?'

'Oh well,' she said. She stopped aimlessly by the kitchen table, smoothing one finger to and fro across the clean white wood, as if a spring had run down. 'But I am pretty tired, darling.'

'I'm somewhat fatigued myself,' said Billy after a moment.

He crossed to the dresser and picked up the whisky bottle and one tumbler. He carried them into the residents' lounge and settled down, lying on the sofa, to watch last year's fight for the Ashes. As he discovered in the morning, Christa went to bed.

6

'Now, ladies?' said Calum Macnair.

'Calum,' said the thin little woman comfortably, and then she gave a start. 'Och, Ellen, I never saw you there. Were you in front of me?'

Fine you know I was, Katie, and you settling down for half-an-hour's blether before you buy your six pork links. 'No, no, Miss Frizell, just go ahead,' said Ellen in her most stately tones. 'You'll be in your usual hurry, and it's the half day.' Kate Frizell flickered a glance round at her which might have been suspicious, except that the woman didn't have that much brains.

'What are your pork links like this morning, Calum?'

'Full of goodness like myself, Kate,' said Calum Macnair with well-practised cheer.

'Well, I wonder now. That would do for our tea, but I was half thinking about something for Mr Frizell's dinner.'

'Take your time, take your time,' said the fat fool, beaming all over his face.

Ellen sighed and shifted her weight to the other foot. Nora Macnair was flitting about behind the counter in her stiff white coat like one of the undead, but eggs and tomatoes were all she was allowed to serve. Bethia Gillespie, young Finlay's mother, came in behind Ellen, assessed the situation, and rested her shopping-bag on the counter rail. 'Ellen,' she said.

Ellen had been quite amused at this unvarying form of greeting, once long ago coming new to Finavay as a bride.

'Bethia,' she said, and looked distantly over Bethia's bird's nest of a head.

'And that's you back from Glasgow then,' remarked Calum Macnair to Kate, as if she might perhaps not have noticed.

'Here!' cried Kate, reminded. She had been on the point of

deciding for beef olives, but we're away, thought Ellen, now. 'Wasn't I walking along Sauchiehall Street, never thinking, and who should I meet but Flora Ferguson!'

Oh, they're on the hunt now, thought Ellen. Now the tongues begin. Down the street she saw a familiar red head, a slim figure moving from shop to shop. You could tell the incomers like Christa; they walked fast, as if there was somewhere to go.

Bethia Gillespie had the impertinence to lean right across Ellen, all cushiony soft and sweet perfume over old sweat, and say to Kate, 'How is she, Flora, the creature?'

'Oh, she puts a good face on it, I'll say that,' said Kate, 'but she's not the woman she was. Och, you couldna expect it after that. She'll never get over it right, no' till the end of her days.'

'A terrible thing thon,' said Calum, deep in his barrel belly. 'A tink, they were saying at the time.'

'Oh, it was a tink all right, and they know the man,' said Bethia importantly, 'but they couldna pin it on him, I suppose.'

'Why would he do a thing like that, and her an old woman?' said Kate, quite pathetic.

'They were saying it would be an old spite he had,' said Calum. 'Maybe she chased him from the door some time.'

'Oh, you couldna put anything past a tink,' said Bethia. 'It was him right enough. My cousin's brother-in-law that's the desk sergeant told us. Big Mackenzie, him they cry the Flounder, went up to the camp with Isa Fraser's Johnny, but a' they got was dog's abuse. But allow the tinks to get out of a thing, the camp was cleared the next day.'

'Terrible altogether,' nodded Calum.

'But they're back!' cried Kate, alarmed that she might have lost the floor. 'Rose Veitch had two of them in the chemist's the day. She near about fainted, she said. Two big toms o' them, bold as brass. An' you wouldna guess —' She drew herself up, primming her lips, and glanced at Bethia, briefly at Ellen, and meaningfully at Calum. 'Rose Veitch could not bring herself,' she enunciated, 'to tell me what they were buying.'

'It wouldna be soap,' said Calum, unabashed.

'Well,' said Kate with finality, 'I'll be locking my door while they're here, I assure you. I'll have six of your pork links, Calum, if you please.'

I don't suppose they'll be breaking in your window, Katie, thought Ellen. Over Bethia's head she saw Christa coming out of the baker's, settling her silly-looking basket on her arm as if she was selling clothespegs. Jean Lambert, puttering past in her little car, wound down the window to call some question to Christa, who typically enough both nodded and shook her head. They conversed in the middle of the road as other motorists steered politely round them. Christa skipped to the pavement and Jean moved on. Well, it's her busy night, thought Ellen. She smiled graciously at Calum, and had her reward. In his smooth fat cheek, mapped with broken veins, a nerve jerked and beat.

Bethia, beached by Kate's sudden decision on the pork links, was looking out of the window now.

'Och, it's Mrs Beresford.'

'That's right,' said Ellen coldly.

'Aye, aye, Chrissie Forrest that was,' said Bethia in mild wonder. 'You'll mind her, Kate, when she would come to stay with old Sarah. You wouldna be in the town yet, Ellen. I suppose she will have the house nearly straight now. I'm hearing from Finlay's Dolina the bedrooms are terrible damp.'

Kate said reprovingly, 'Miss Forrest wasna fit for it this last year and more. It's a wonder she had any bookings for the summer at all, for I'm sure she was in hospital by the turn of the year.'

'Och, they book ahead,' said Calum the businessman, making a neat parcel of the pork links. 'They'll have their wallets out right hearty paying a big deposit, and enquiring casual-like in the by-going will they get it at last year's price. She fell on her feet there did Chrissie, the house an' the goodwill an' all.'

'I suppose it was willed to her father,' said Kate with the authority of a solicitor's sister, 'and she's just got it to see can she make a go of it this year.'

'I wonder will she,' said Bethia, hopeful of grief.

'It's lucky the two of them could both up and leave their jobs,' said Calum, 'whatever it was they did at all.'

'Lucky,' agreed Bethia consideringly, and 'Lucky right enough,' mused Kate Frizell, and they all watched with interest as Christa, long legs and wicker basket and swift incomer's walk, crossed the street, making for the chemist's. As she passed the butcher's she saw Ellen, and cheerfully waved. Ellen, accepting the greeting for herself alone, graciously raised her hand.

No surprise but Kate and Bethia would make her pay for that. 'You'll be well set there, Ellen,' whispered Bethia out of her fat face. 'Better than the manse, anyway now.'

'Och yes, you were right to hand in your notice, Ellen,' said Kate, sharp as a stoat. 'It wouldna have been the same hardly, and the new one a married man.'

Ellen kept her face straight, though the heat came to her cheekbones. She saw the two bitches in simpering accord, and that fat old goat getting his kicks from it, but not for the world or his wife would she let on. Wouldn't it be great, just one time, to come right out! Don't make a meal of it, ladies, it only happened the once. And as a matter of fact, she could say, drawling it out in Christa's affected style, as a matter of *fact* it didn't happen, and the man was black ashamed, and some way we just went on as we'd been —

'She's a decent wee soul is Chrissie,' she said from a great height. 'She hasn't her sorrows to seek right enough, but I will say he's never seen the worse for it outside.'

She drew her brows together in a preoccupied way and gave her attention to the trays of meat.

'Oh dear me,' she heard Kate twitter in joy. 'A fine-looking lad like that too!'

'Aye, but he's got a bit of a look of it though,' nodded Bethia. 'It doesna take long before you can be seeing the signs.'

'Was I not thinking the same myself,' said Calum, 'only on Sunday there?' He leaned his huge forearms on the counter, entirely abandoning his trade. 'I happened to call in on my road past, just in a neighbourly way, and here wasna the bottle out already, hardly five o'clock in the day. He poured me a good dram right enough,' he said judicially, 'but I wish you would see the couple he poured for himself.'

'I believe I'll have one of your chickens today, Calum,' said Ellen, 'that's if you have got all you were wanting, Miss Frizell?'

'I was half thinking about a quarter of bacon, sweet cure,' said Kate, but she didn't press the point. There was more, thought Ellen as with a smile she completed her business, to occupy her tiny mind.

7

At one o'clock Calum pulled down his blinds on the suddenly quiet street. Half day closing, and the town had died. 'Aye,aye,' he said,as usual, 'another day in.' He went into the back shop to throw his bloodstained white coat into the laundry bin, and came out to cash up. Nora, as usual, was taking fistfuls of notes out of the till.

He stood heavily and looked at her. He had long ago run through all the reasonable things to say. She felt him looking and her thin face wrinkled up in a fixed crocodile grin.

'How much have ye got the day?'

'No' much,' she whined like a tink. 'It'll never be missed.'

It had started with pound notes, but he could see fives and tens at least in her hand. She closed her fist defensively over the money and scuttled away from him into the toilet. She even snibbed the door, though surely to God after thirty years she should know he'd never follow her in there. She always came out walking stiff and erect like Queen Mary. Where she stowed the money he didn't want to know.

They drove home in silence through the deathly sunny streets of the closed-down town. The small house, shut since early morning, stank of unmentionable things. He went round opening windows, and that gave her the chance to get the money out of her drawers. He came back into the living-room to find her stuffing notes into a vase. 'There's no necessity for that, Nora,' he said wearily. 'There's money in the bank yet. You've only to ask.'

She peeked round the moth-eaten fur collar of the coat that even in this warm June weather she wouldn't put off. 'But what do I do when ye leave me?' she cunningly said.

He sighed. 'Nora,' he said, 'I'm not going to leave you.'

'You leave me every Thursday!' she shrieked. 'Forbye Sunday nights!'

'I aye come back.'

'When it suits ye,' she hissed.

'I wouldna leave you, Nora,' he said, despairing in the little stuffy room. 'I've told ye an' I've better told ye. Can ye no' believe me?'

'I'll believe ye when ye stop going to that wumman.'

'A man's got tae have some relaxation!' he yelled.

They looked at one another in horror, then a smile spread over her face, satisfied, dreadful, pleased.

'So there it's out at last,' she said. 'Oh aye, it's right enough, you're a' the same. That's a' you ever think about.'

He felt his fingers crook ready for her neck. He screamed, feeling the big vein pulse in his brow, 'You, ye bitch, you never think about it at all!'

He couldn't stay in the same room with her after that. He blundered away to the bathroom and, shaking, washed his face and his hacked, blood-engrained fat hands. When he went back to the living-room she wasn't there, and she had taken the money out of the vase. He banged out of the house without even a cup of tea, because he knew he would get a good meal at Jean's.

8

The lady in the chemist's hadn't seemed so funny today. Ten days ago Christa and Billy had nearly disgraced themselves, going in together to buy odds and ends: 'Oh, and Tampax,' Christa added. 'Pass it over, would you, darling?'

Unfortunately this caused Miss Veitch untold embarrassment. She didn't know where to look as with pink-patched cheeks and stiff fingers she received the box from Billy's hand. She proceeded to wrap it up while pretending it wasn't there; the thick flannelly brown paper wouldn't stay creased, springing apart, disclosing its shameful contents again and again. Billy was standing elbow to elbow with Christa, and she felt him begin to shake with laughter so much that she was forced to send him on an imaginary errand out to the car.

That should have ended in a rather nice evening; only they came home to Glenrosa. Out of the car into the dusty twilight under the crowding heavy dark-green leaves: 'I think we'll have to cut those back,' she said. It all came over her on the word, the big strange house, a load of work waiting, responsibility, an end to mirth. 'I wonder whether Ellen and Dolina remembered to air the bedrooms,' she said, pulling away from Billy's encircling arm.

They had, but the chilly, unwelcoming big rooms still smelt of ancient damp. Christa came back gloomily to the owner's flat, and once again Billy's best efforts met with very little response.

Since then there had been the business of Hughie Macafee, making matters rather worse.

Miss Rose Veitch had been well up to standard today too: 'It's terrible, Mrs Beresford, the things I'm expected to sell.' Her eyes fluttered despite herself towards the little packets so handily displayed beside the till. 'And the worst of it is, they go like hot cakes.' Christa didn't know what Billy might have said at this point, or whether they would have looked at each other and fled the shop again. She suddenly and quite desperately wanted him beside her, laughing or not, unregenerate, alive. She couldn't find the energy even to be really amused. 'That's life,' she listlessly said.

Everything was a bit of a chore today. Though it was no distance from the shops up to Glenrosa, Christa wished she'd brought the car. The hot June roads shimmered under a deep blue sky. 'The visitors will love it,' she could almost hear Jean say. She wouldn't have minded Jean's company, unexciting, capable, calm. But after a few words in the middle of the street Jean had slapped the car into gear and called 'Must go, afternoon off—'. She hadn't suggested another picnic. The way I went on, Christa thought with a memory twinge, she'll probably never ask me again.

Two days, and everything still to do. She dumped her heavy basket on the kitchen table: relax, relax. Thanks mainly to Ellen the floor gleamed, the fire crackled hot in the Aga, well-risen cakes were cooling on their racks. In the kitchen things could be predicted and organized. Up on the first-floor landing Linnet and Dolina were squabbling again.

'She said pink sheets for the side room—'Dolina was doggedly repeating.

'She didn't mean those pink sheets,' came Linnet's irritating, teasing voice 'because they're double ones.'

'Well, you can put double sheets on a single bed.'

'Then you end up with no double sheets for the double beds.'

'Just because you're at the Uni, Linnet O'Connell—'

'Well, they're marked, look, D for dumb —'

'Oh, and S for stupid I suppose,' said Dolina with unusual venom.

Christa ran upstairs calling 'What's the trouble, girls?' If I've said those words, she thought, once this week -'We have pink double and pink single, Dolina,' she said. 'All the single sheets should be in the same pile, that's if they were put away properly.'

'Linnet put them away,' said Dolina with satisfaction.

'Only the double ones,' said Linnet smartly, 'because don't you remember —'

Christa extracted a pair of pink single sheets from the wrong pile and placed them in Dolina's arms. 'Side room,' she said. 'Linnet, what's that on the sheet you're holding? I think it's a long brown hair.'

Dolina smugly tossed her short dark curls. Linnet carefully picked up the hair and examined it back and front. 'You got me bang to rights, boss,' she said.

'Well, you'll have to tie it up. I've told you and told you.'

'After the beds?' suggested the obliging Linnet.

'Before.'

'Okey-dokey,' said Linnet. She laid her sheet over the banister, which had yet to be dusted, and from the pocket of her striped apron drew a piece of bristly string. 'I kept this off the grocer's box specially, but then I forgot I had it,' she explained as she gathered and tied. Christa observed that on each of her long, well-shaped fingernails she had painted a little smiling face.

Ellen surely hadn't seen that yet. 'Your auntie,' Ellen had remarked in her helpful way, 'always had her girls in black frocks and white aprons.' Christa had said blithely, 'Oh, as long as they're clean —' It then turned out that Linnet always wore denims, and Dolina always wore extremely low-cut summer dresses with frilly petticoats underneath, all immaculately clean, indeed, because they turned up daily in the household wash. Christa felt, not for the first time, that the house would run very smoothly with Ellen in charge.

Dolina was still preening herself on having short hair, and she hadn't taken one step towards the side room. 'And you,

Dolina,' said Christa in unreasonable irritation, 'you've got that strong perfume on again.'

'It's my patchouli,' said Dolina, sticking out her lip.

'Not everybody likes patchouli all over their sheets,' said Christa, 'and you certainly mustn't wear it when you're serving the tables. I've told you and —'

She stopped, hearing the edge of hysteria in her voice. I wonder, she thought, if I am going to be able to stand this. Dolina's round cheeks were even pinker than usual, her long dark eyelashes hid her eyes, and she still hadn't moved an inch.

'Dolina's in an incredible sulk,' said Linnet.

'Dolina to the side room, Linnet to the west wing,' said Christa with her last breath of energy. She waited until, with their armfuls of linen, they were slowly moving to their posts. She went downstairs into the hall, and then up to the owner's flat, where she sat down on the sofa and burst into tears.

Billy came out of the bathroom, half-shaved, and wrapped her in his arms. 'Well,' he said presently, 'it'll save me having a bath.'

Christa laughed and sobbed and rubbed her eyes with the heels of her hands. 'I thought you'd be in with the telly,' she said.

'It's Postman Pat and I've seen it twice,' said Billy. 'Darling, if it's as bad as all that we needn't go on.'

'We must, it's Thursday, they come on Saturday -'

'You're not going to see Saturday unless you take a break now. Anything special wrong?'

'No, just Dolina and Linnet, they don't get on, Linnet teases Dolina and Dolina sulks —'

'Situation normal,' said Billy. He picked up the car keys, ran a thumb resignedly over his chin, and scooped Christa off the sofa. On their way to the side door they heard Dolina and Linnet coming downstairs; at least Dolina was coming, announcing loudly that she needed a cup of coffee if nobody else did. Linnet had stopped on the landing by the staircase window, gazing out in rapture, as she tended to do, at Finavay Bay in its summer sleep and the grape-blue hills beyond. 'Just blacklead the range and wash all the curtains while we're out,' called Billy. Christa giggled damply at the glimpse of their astonished faces, caught in a momentary likeness, mouths ajar.

'Oh, darling, I don't deserve it, but you've rescued me again.'

'I'm extremely forgiving. I think it's a day for the hill,' said Billy, turning out of the gate without any great care. They all but clipped a car on its law-abiding way up the chapel road, and its driver raised a hand in ironical salute. 'Road-hog,' said Billy pleasantly.

'I think that was the Catholic priest.'

'Jesus,' said Billy, 'we nearly needed him.' They both giggled childishly. Christa leaned her head on Billy's shoulder, blissfully tired in the aftermath of tears. He glanced down at her with a grin. 'When I nod, you change gear,' he said.

And it was lovely on Finavay Hill. Even since Sunday the summer had moved on, the bracken uncurled to its green height and strength, the heart-shaped birch leaves flickering shadows over the road. They had the top down and Christa lay back in the scented air, watching Billy's long hands gentle on the wheel. He was a good driver, though he was too lazy to go fast or far. Their first spring together, imbued with the energy of new love, they had driven for miles by back roads and byways, talking, not talking. Christa stole a look at Billy's profile: she used to do the same then, wondering where they were going, in more senses than one. As then, his dark-browed blue eyes slid from the road to meet hers with a wicked spark. His fair-brown hair, feathering in the hill breeze, was streaked across his brow, the way it was in the mornings. Oh, God, she thought, it's not where we are going now, darling, but where we've been.

Because that early spring shimmered into another one, only months ago by the calendar, in a different age of the world. They had gone out driving again: she was heavy and restless and couldn't settle in a chair. He had looked down at her then and her body answered as strongly as ever, quite independent, it seemed, of its load.

'Are you sure it's all right, though, darling?' he said.

'It's been weeks,' she said, 'it's been months —'

'I know,' he said, caressing the stretched skin, so thin a barrier between him and his son. And she saw him as urgent as herself, and it didn't take much more persuading. Her mind blinked like a camera shutter, closing off what happened after that. Though the image was preserved.

But up on the blue and green and shining hill she thought that perhaps it was over at last. On its way from gear-lever to steering-wheel his left hand, with the slightest tremble in its long fingers, rested for a tentative moment on her knee. She found she didn't mind. She put her hand over his, and he glanced sharply at her in case she was pushing him away; but she tightened her grip, and he relaxed and smiled at her.

'It's nice being married to you,' she said.

'In some ways?' he ventured to say.

'In all ways,' she said, and raised the back of his hand to her cheek. He began to look round for a good place to stop.

'The road ends just a bit ahead.'

'Right,' he said, and retrieved his hand to change gear. He began to whistle as he drove carefully on. She wondered if he knew what he was whistling. He knew certainly, from long ago, how that song made her feel.

> 'The water is wide . . .
> I cannot get o'er . . .
> And neither have I wings to fly
> Give me a boat . . .
> that will carry two . . .
> And both shall row —'

He broke off to ask 'Do we go through here?'

They had come to the gate that Christa had opened for Jean on the way to the tinkers' camp. Standing on its bars and sitting on the fence-posts were half-a-dozen dirty children in faded, ragged jerseys, with long brown legs and orange tinker hair, lithe and cheeky as squirrels, chewing on buttered rolls. Down among the threadbare stained skirts and trousers, peering through the gate, there was surely a round baby face under a quiff of tow-rough hair. As the children jumped down and ran away Christa saw a flash of red.

'Christa, what the hell?'

She was out of the car before it had properly stopped, and over the gate, though her skirt wasn't the right shape for climbing. A little girl had dropped her roll and stopped to pick it up. Christa was on her like a pouncing owl, catching her by the chicken-bone shoulders before she could get away.

'In the red jersey? Was it Hughie?'

'Lea' us alane!'

'I'm not going to hurt you! I'm only —' What on earth am I doing? Standing knee-deep in wet bracken with a screaming tinker child kicking my legs; but no use stopping now. 'I'm only asking if that was Hughie Macafee?'

The little girl all of a sudden changed her tune to the ingratiating tinker lilt. 'D'ye want 'im, lady?'

'I wanted to — I thought —'

'Hughie Toilet!' yelled the little girl.

'Hughie Toilet, Hughie Toilet!' wailed merry voices farther away.

'Christa —' Billy was at her side.

The tinker child pulled on her arm with shrewish strength. At the bend of the path the other children were jumping up and down shouting 'Hughie Toilet! The wumman wants ye!' There were the tents and the fire under their greening cliff, and the old van evidently undergoing repairs, for a man was lying underneath it, only a long pair of denimed legs sticking out. Hughie was there sure enough: he fled in alarm from the sight of Christa and dived for cover beneath the van. The man started, banged his head, and wriggled clear, hauling Hughie out with the slack of his jersey wrapped round a dirty fist.

'See you, ya wee —'

'No, don't!' screamed Christa.

Instantly the startled children went quiet. Hughie's father, ruffled and oil-stained, lifted Hughie like a puppy by seat and scruff and stood him squarely on his feet. 'Were ye wanting tae see him, missis?' he said.

'I was just passing —' She really didn't know what to say next. I took a notion, she'd heard Dolina say. 'I was here on Sunday with Nurse Lambert,' she said. It didn't seem to explain very much.

'So ye were!' said Hughie's father in some amusement, and dragged his cigarettes from his back pocket.

Billy said shortly, 'Have one of mine.'

Christa had forgotten he was there. It didn't seem right that he was. The business of Hughie was none of his; nothing that he could be expected to feel. 'I'll tell you when we get home,' she said over her shoulder.

'Well, thanks a bunch,' Billy said.

She knelt down on the dusty ground and held out her hands. Hughie wanted to run, but there was nowhere to go: the circle of children had closed around them, and directly in his way of escape loomed his father's long legs. He stood drawn into himself, sucking his thumb, clutching for courage at the front of his small trousers. Now he was as dirty as any of the children, and his fair hair needed a wash, and in the shoulder of his red jersey there was a big unravelling tear.

'Is he all right?' said Christa, looking up at his father.

'Fine, ach, fine altogether,' said the young man heartily.

Hughie's saucer eyes swivelled in his head, searching out

a tone that he didn't quite understand. 'The lady's wanting ye, Hughie,' said his father. 'Over ye go, g'wan.' Hughie stood rooted to his patch of ground and his father made a move towards him. Under his shadow Hughie flinched away.

'Don't!' cried Christa again, and snatched Hughie into her arms.

In his extremity he burrowed his face into her neck, into the warm place that it exactly fitted, where it belonged. He smelt strongly now of the tinkers' tent, but he was still a round warm little boy. She held him fiercely close with her cheek hard against his unkempt hair. She heard Billy say behind her 'Oh Christa, love.' She couldn't think why he should sound so unlike himself.

From the tents Theresa's harsh rich voice said 'It's awful nice o' ye to take an interest in the wee fella.'

She came forward like a queen, but her bright eyes never rested, darting alertly from Christa to Billy to Hughie, and back to Christa again. She settled her shawl around her shoulders and beamed at them, a devoted grandmother, loving and concerned. 'You've nae family o' yer ain, lady?' she very pleasantly asked.

Billy lifted Hughie out of Christa's arms and set him on the ground. She didn't resist. She was in deep water: she watched, she couldn't move. Billy held the little boy in sure and gentle hands that knew of themselves what to do.

That was only a blink of a thought. Next moment Hughie was plunging past his father and making for the tents, and Billy, gripping Christa's arm, had pulled her by main force back round the bend in the path.

'Why —?' she gasped in anger and loss.

'She was going to do the wee boy up in a parcel for us,' said Billy curtly. 'That's why.'

'How can you say that!'

He didn't even answer. He helped her over the gate, but

not to the car. She followed him, stumbling, round the side of the hill. Her heart was going like a drum. 'What if she had?' she sobbed. 'What if she had?' He stopped and pulled her down to sit in a nest of bracken, keeping his arm round her in a desperate uncertain grip. She locked her hands round her knees and hunched up, burying her face in her arms. Somewhere above on the hill the cuckoo called, but stammering, comic, its pure note cracked.

She could feel him beside her, wanting to help, bitterly scared that he might make things worse. Of course he hadn't an idea what was really wrong. How could he, when she didn't know?

At last he said, picking his way, 'That old lady's bad medicine.' He bit his thumbnail. 'Did I go over the top?' She didn't speak. 'But did you see their faces when they looked at her? Even the guy. The kids were frozen in their tracks. The bloody birds went quiet.'

'You're imagining it.' Yet he saw that kind of thing sometimes, quite without trying: if he smelt brimstone, you could confidently look for the horns. Christa raised her weary head. 'She's all right really,' she said. 'She's Hughie's granny, that's all. The guy's his father. I saw them on Sunday, you see.'

'Was that where Jean took you? To see that baby?'

Christa could only nod.

'Jesus wept,' said Billy savagely. '*What* a stupid bitch.' He caught Christa's startled look. 'Jean, not you,' he said, but he didn't smile.

'Not her fault.' said Christa, desperate and light. 'She doesn't know. I haven't told her yet.' Predictably her voice wavered and failed. 'I can't — I've never been able to—'

'Oh, my love.'

His eyes were dark with concern. As in the car, now in the green bracken his hand was on her knee, smoothing upwards, stroking and moving in. He turned to her, pressing her backwards into the crisp green stems: and now he did begin to smile a little, a tentative smile that steadied and grew sure. He was pleased with himself, Christa thought. He saw what to do, what she wanted and needed, what would make everything all right. His head dropped and he was kissing the hollow of her throat, his hands slipping down her body, urging hard—

But it wasn't all right. It didn't make things right. It meant pain, on and on, and blackness and sickness and hope, and then the storm, the storm of grief —

She flung sideways and rolled over, and lay there panting, curled into a ball, hugging her knees against her breasts.

Billy pushed himself up from the bracken and sat back on his heels.

'Do you want to go down then?' he said.

'Yes, please.'

He drove down the rutted track with exquisite care, feeling his way from gear to gear as if he expected the engine to burst into tears. Some men, she thought numbly, after that, would take it out on the car. But she knew better than anyone in the world how delicate was the skin of his self-confidence over the nerves and feelings below. She had damaged it before; you did when you were married, sometimes intentionally, sometimes not. He must be just and no more holding together, nursing the car so attentively down the hill road into Finavay; because she had flayed him now.

9

On Friday morning, getting ready for the last frantic pre-visitor day, Linnet tied her hair back and remembered to put on her overall, in case Mrs Beresford was going to be a neurotic female boss. The unpredictable creature, however, wasn't too bad. She was extremely brisk and threw herself about as if she was on piecework, but on the whole let other people alone. Mr Beresford helped with furniture-moving, though only when asked. He was as pleasant and decorous as a boss's husband could be. Linnet played it cool.

On Thursday when they'd come back from their drive, after the car had been silently put away and Christa had gone to cry in the bath, he had come into the kitchen, and he'd been very pleasant then too. He had conversed about this and that, university and careers and teaching and Linnet's love-life, while absentmindedly pouring himself a powerful dram. Somewhere between the garage and the kitchen, it became clear, he had already lowered one or two. 'I don't think you ought to handle the help, Mr Beresford,' Linnet eventually observed. He didn't act either offended or ashamed, just grinned and said, 'I don't suppose I should, Miss O'Connell,' and wandered off. Possibly to handle Dolina, but Dolina wouldn't object. Dolina had also put on her overall this morning, but left it lavishly unbuttoned half-way down the front in hopeful mood.

Anyway this morning nothing was being handled but furniture, since Mrs Beresford was everywhere at once, whipping around in a kind of scorpion dance, impressively ready to sting. Mrs Macleod, enough to cool anyone's ardour in her straight-up-and-down black overall, unbent enough to say 'How did you manage to move the dining tables on your own, girls?'

'We strove,' said Linnet, 'mightily.' She did wonder what dim schoolgirl code persuaded her not to add 'And of course Finlay was a great help.' Dolina had phoned Finlay as soon as the car turned out of the gate, and after the short sharp burst of table-moving Linnet had peacefully read her book in the residents' lounge. How much had gone on up the back stairs she wasn't sure. There was Dolina the childish, awkward, sulky little school-leaver; but also, even since Sunday, she had met the Dolina drenched in patchouli, with the wrong colour of lipstick, coming in at night to sit on Linnet's bed and tell stories that would have made the rugby club blink.

'Well, now let's strive to get finished,' said Mrs Beresford, pretty sharp. 'They come tomorrow, don't forget.'

So they polished the front hall and cleaned the loos yet again and dusted everything in sight, and sank down at last for elevenses on the front doorstep in the sun. Christa flopped down exhausted too, no wonder, and Billy joined them, impeccably courteous to everyone, including his wife. You would hardly know that he had been so diligently hitting the bottle, and except for hearing her in the bath last night, Linnet would probably never have noticed Christa's eyelids. At her age she couldn't be expected to be quick in shedding the puffiness of tears.

Mrs Macleod had brought out a camp-stool. Linnet tried, but failed, to imagine her sprawled leggily on the steps. She sat upright and efficient as if she was chairing a meeting, and said, 'Oh, Mrs Beresford, I spoke to Mr Cowan about the grocer's account. He will send your order every Friday, but would you please phone him on the Thursday if there's anything to add.'

'Or subtract,' said Christa brightly.

'I don't think he gives house-room to that possibility,' said Mrs Macleod. Sometimes, thought Linnet, you would almost suspect the woman had humour in her.

'What about paying?'

'I have the details indoors,' said Mrs Macleod with a stern and meaningful look at the girls.

'You could run this business, Ellen,' said Christa, laughing.

'Yes,' said Mrs Macleod, as far from a smile as ever, 'so I could.'

Linnet could see her doing it, too: the overall and dust-scarf had the right off-hand air, as if she kept the tiara on the dresser for evenings. She leaned forward and said eagerly, 'Was that what you did before you were married, Mrs Macleod?'

'No.' Perhaps that sounded a trifle abrupt even to the self-composed Ellen: she added, 'I didn't train for any job. I lived up the glen and you were supposed to – anyway I married straight from school.'

'Oh, that would be right romantic,' sighed Dolina. 'Was he a Finavay man then?'

'A fisherman.'

'Watch it, Dolina, they're fast workers those seafaring men,' Linnet cried.

'My husband was drowned not very long afterwards,' said Ellen. Linnet felt herself go scarlet: foot in mouth *again* . . . When her ears stopped ringing with embarrassment, Ellen Macleod was saying 'And with Mairi to bring up, I just took casual work where I could.'

You couldn't imagine her ever being casual about anything. Linnet looked at her properly for the first time, putting her against a backcloth of romance and tragedy, dust-scarf and all. When you worked it out, she couldn't be very much older than Mrs Beresford. Beside her Christa was a scatty girl. Ellen's dark, high-boned face, so rarely lightened by its slow considering smile, was full of intelligence and pride. Sure, chairperson of the board, no problem, Linnet thought; but for once she managed not to say it aloud.

'Will you want any lunch?' said Christa politely to Billy as they got up to start work again.

'No, don't bother,' he said, picking up the whisky bottle from the dresser. 'There's show-jumping this afternoon.'

'Dinner?'

'Depends what you have to offer,' said Billy with the utmost cordiality. Colour whipped into Christa's face and she said tonelessly, 'I'll ask you later then.' Billy raised his bottle in smiling acknowledgment. It looked to Linnet very much as if he hoped to be spark out on the sofa by the time dinner was served.

Christa pulled herself together and addressed her staff brightly. 'We've broken the back of it now, girls. Another hour or so should do it, and we can take the rest of the day off.'

'Lovely!' cried Linnet. I wonder what you'll find to do with it, boss, she wanted to say.

But Christa was good at planning, and you could see everything slotting into place, down to the very flower-vases ready in the pantry to be filled tomorrow morning. Billy's jacket and a pair of Dolina's shoes were removed from the cloakroom where only visitors' garments had the right to be. A note of mealtimes was posted in the dining-room. Towels and soap at washbasins, open the bedroom windows one more time, wind up the old clock in the hall: 'I do believe we're ready,' Christa said.

It was like the last school bell of term. Linnet punched the air and embraced Dolina footballer-style. Dolina giggled till the tears ran down her round pink cheeks. Mrs Macleod raised her eyes to heaven, especially when the pair of them fell over a table and brought it crashing to the floor.

'I think this table is trying to tell us something,' said Linnet, picking herself up.

'It helps if you look the way you're going,' observed Mrs Macleod.

But Christa was laughing too, stern and boss-like intentions set aside. 'It shouldn't be in the hall really. Linnet, can you -?'

'Watch me,' said Linnet, heaving it into her arms. It was a light little table with a round polished top, not meant for any serious use. 'Where? Owner's flat?'

'The kitchen will do just now,' said Christa absently. 'I think I'll — I'd better —'

And what had shut her up so suddenly? Oh yes, thought Linnet. Now they had stopped bustling and fooling around; the television booming from the residents' lounge, and the sound of Billy changing channels, dissatisfied restless clicks. Christa went there without a word. If I was a praying person, this would be the moment, Linnet thought.

'Okay, Dolina, can you open the door?'

They put the table down in the middle of the kitchen floor. 'I can't believe that's where she meant, exactly,' said Linnet. 'Still. So far so good. Now for a touch of the table-turning.' With her overall sleeve she briskly rubbed up the little table's shining top.

'What d'you mean? It wouldn't turn,' said the literal Dolina. 'See, the top and the bottom's all one.'

'No, but you know, the thing with the tumbler. Spirit of the glass. It's just right, this table. Round ones work best.'

'You're droll, Linnet O'Connell.'

'Well, if you don't want to know your fate —'

Naturally Dolina was hooked. With a kitchen tumbler and a couple of corners torn off the calendar, they were in business in a small way. Linnet printed Yes and No on the scraps of paper, and Dolina was most impressed by the way the spirit knew all about Finlay. Linnet felt a bit rotten, but it was quite a challenge, pushing the glass with her fingertip hard enough to make it move as required, yet not so hard as to shatter Dolina's girlish illusions. Concentrating on this task, she didn't hear Mrs Macleod come in with her notes about the grocer's bill.

'What on earth are you doing, girls?'

Linnet jumped and said with a grin, '*Cave*, here comes the Head.' Unfortunately Mrs Macleod wasn't amused; and even more unfortunately, Dolina was too excited to take a warning.

'Oh, Mrs Macleod, it's great fun! It's spooky! We're getting messages!'

'Messages?' said Mrs Macleod. Not amused, oh dear, very little amused, Linnet could see. 'Who from?'

'Tell her, Linnet, say what you said to me —'

Linnet really did feel by now that they had been caught at larks in the dorm. Sheepishly she put on her sepulchral voice and said 'From the dead . . .'. It wasn't well received.

'Linnet, I don't think that is a thing to be joking about.'

'No, I know, we were only —'

'It's very dangerous playing with matters like that. You're older than Dolina, you're supposed to be an educated girl, you should know better.'

'It's only —'

'Put those things away this minute and don't let me —'

'Ellen,' said Christa quite quietly from the door.

Her face was pink in the wrong places, and again there was that trace of tears about her eyes. She looked ready for a bust-up, and with Ellen too; Linnet nervously looked round for shelter from the breaking storm.

It didn't break. Christa put her shoulders back and took a deep breath. 'Table-turning, are you?' she said. 'It's only fun, Ellen, you know.'

Dolina proved herself to be totally without sense. 'Have you done it, Mrs Beresford?' she chirped.

'Oh, when I was a student,' said Christa. She was speaking at random, pushing back her untidy hair. 'But somebody got hysterical and we were told to stop.'

'Did you get messages, then?'

'I'm sure it was somebody kidding.'

'But you did get messages!' squeaked Dolina.

Ellen said politely, 'I don't think it's just a very good thing to be playing with, Mrs Beresford. I was telling the girls —'

'I heard you,' said Christa.

Take cover, here they go; but Christa sighed and rubbed her eyes. 'Sorry,' she said. She looked at the little table. 'That tumbler's rather heavy,' she said. 'A thinner one slides better. And we used to have the twenty-six letters as well as Yes and No.'

'Mrs Beresford,' said Ellen.

Christa's red-haired temper was high; but nothing to do with you, Ellen, Linnet gloomily thought. 'It's only fun, I told you.' She was over at the dresser now, searching for the right kind of glass. She picked up a whisky tumbler and ran her finger along its precise engraved design. 'At least I think it was fun,' she said. She seemed to be somewhere else; somewhere they hadn't been. 'I haven't done it,' she continued, 'since I was married.'

'Would Mr Beresford approve?' Ellen said.

It was a shame for Christa with her redhead's delicate skin: the colour splashed across her cheekbones again, however insouciant her words. 'You don't really believe in it, surely?' she said. 'Linnet, you cut up the letters, will you? Come on, Ellen, be a sport. Just one turn. Dolina will never rest now till we do.'

And neither will Christa, thought Linnet. Ellen might have known.

On a sheet of Christa's auntie's best notepaper she busily printed the letters of the alphabet, and looked around for scissors. Well, I hadn't better rig it this time. Best if it doesn't work at all.

Ellen was pulling up a chair, sitting down at the little round table, folding back her overall sleeves. Reluctance was in her every move. Her eyes, hidden under their heavy lids, gleamed for just a moment as they flickered to Christa's determined bright face. Damn me, thought Linnet; Ellen did know.

10

In the cavernous great kitchen they sat round the little table, a self-conscious, nervous bunch; but Linnet, who seemed to have taken on the priestess role, calmed them down. 'It doesn't always work, you know,' she said.

'Och, Linnet, you said I'd get a message!'

'I hope you'll like it if you do,' said Ellen tartly.

We're all daft, Christa thought. But sillier still to back out now. 'Doesn't work if you scoff at it,' she said. 'That I do remember.' She laid her finger on the upturned glass, beside Ellen's long brown finger, and Dolina's bitten-down nail, and Linnet's slender finger painted with its cheerful little face. 'Serious now, everybody. Shh.'

Linnet's hair, which never stayed up for long, fell across her absorbed young profile as she leaned over the table. Dolina was keeping quiet with an effort that you could feel. The kitchen clock ticked, one, two, three, in the silent spaces of the room.

'The spirit knows our secret thoughts,' said Linnet in an unaccustomed gentle voice. 'Think of someone you want to hear from.'

And Christa thought: What if I do hear from him?

Under their fingers the glass gave a shiver and then was still.

'Who was that? Who pushed it?' cried Dolina.

Linnet looked up in surprise. 'Don't press too hard, Dolina. Just the lightest touch. That's it.'

Christa controlled with an effort the tremor in her arm. What if I do? Will he blame me? How could he? He's too young to understand . . . She thought, I should draw out now. To the others it's only fun. Dolina was stifling giggles. You couldn't tell what Ellen was thinking, but of course you never could. She said in her mind to the baby who had so bravely kicked and turned, 'The doctors said it was nothing we did.' The wild night; and it wasn't Billy's fault –

Across the table Linnet's clear eyes met Christa's for the briefest moment. She remembers, she knows. Under the hair and inside the kookiness an unexpected Linnet sat there, looking down once more, concentrating on the glass. Oh, damn her, she's being kind.

'I've got a feeling it's not going to work,' Linnet said.

'It is so working! Sure we felt it moving! Say what you said before!'

Linnet bent her head over the second-best whisky tumbler and said with a sigh, 'Spirit of the glass, are you there?'

Nothing happened at all.

'Try it again, sure you said it has a long way to come —'

'Spirit of the glass, are you there?'

No movement, no vibration.

'Ach to hell, Linnet, say it the way you said it before.'

Linnet sighed again, and said, deep and gentle, 'Spirit of the glass, we are friendly towards you.'

There was the slightest shivering rattle on the smooth polished wood.

'Spirit of the glass, are you there?'

Slowly, hesitantly, yet definite and self-willed under their unbelieving fingertips, the glass moved across the table and stopped before the card saying YES.

'Oh Dhia -' cried Dolina.

'Ellen, should we stop now?'

But Ellen was staring in fascination at the glass, and Linnet was going on.

'Spirit of the glass, we're glad to meet you. Are you going to speak to us?'

The glass drew away slightly and moved back to YES.

'Will you tell us your name?'

NO.

'Oh well, we'll tell you ours. I'm Linnet -'

'Dolina,' came a scared whisper.

'Ellen.'

'Christa,' breathed Christa; and as she spoke the glass shivered once more under their fingers, moved away, and with neat delicate movements from letter to letter round the table spelled out: H-E-L-L-O.

They smiled at each other nervously, yet the atmosphere had lightened. That didn't sound like what you'd call a message from the dead. So get a grip on yourself, Christa thought, looking from face to face. Who was pushing the glass? Not Dolina, sitting there pink-cheeked and bright-eyed like a child on Christmas Eve. Was Linnet the rascal, behind that solemn fagade? It couldn't possibly - could it? - be Ellen?

SPEAK, the glass firmly said.

'Oh, sorry,' said Linnet. 'May we ask more about you? Thank you. Spirit of the glass, are you a man?'

NO, said the glass with an extremely definite move.

'A woman?'

YES, said the glass, and under their incredulous eyes added: SILLY.

Even the priestess giggled. 'I see what she means,' said Ellen. When order was restored Linnet said, 'You've quite put me off. Let's see — Oh yes, this is one we used to ask. Are you happy where you are?'

YES.

Ellen said unexpectedly, 'Where's that?'

'I'm not sure we're allowed to ask that,' ventured Christa.

'Still, I would like to know,' said Ellen. She leaned forward and said 'Are you a good spirit?' The glass ran irritably round in small circles. 'Oh, I didn't mean to offend you,' said Ellen, raising her brows.

Linnet gave her a grin. That settles it, Christa thought.

She's pleased to see Ellen's been won over. It's been Linnet all along.

And Linnet was speaking again: 'Spirit of the glass, have you a message for anyone here?'

YES.

Dolina and Christa snatched their fingers away from the glass as if they had been burned. Ellen laughed gently, keeping hers steady, and said 'You that doesn't believe in it, Mrs Beresford?' Christa after a moment put her finger back on with the utmost delicacy, ready to identify the slightest pressure, from wherever it might come.

'Spirit of the glass,' said Linnet, having soothed the over-excited Dolina, 'who is your message for?'

D-O-L-L-

'If you mean Dolina,' said Christa in nervous haste, 'there's only one L.'

YES DOLINA, the glass said.

'Oh no! Oh mammy!'

'What's the message for Dolina?'

MARRY.

A marked change came over Dolina: she preened, she secretly smiled. Linnet was grinning broadly now. Oh, you rotter, Linnet, Christa thought.

'You speak to her, Dolina,' Linnet urged.

Dolina leaned forward and said 'Spirit of the glass -'She couldn't get the words out for giggling. The glass waited courteously. 'Spirit of the glass,' she finally managed to say, 'who is't I'm going to marry?'

NICE BOY, the glass encouragingly said.

Dolina giggled till her eyes were lost in her pink face. 'Is it—is it Finlay?' she bubbled.

NO.

'Oh.'

The glass wouldn't say who Dolina would marry. It offered

Linnet only NICE BOY. When Christa cunningly enquired, 'Who will I marry?' the glass whirled round the table, nearly out of control. 'She doesn't like trick questions,' said Linnet sternly. She had taken on the air of a protector, truly a medium between the spirit and themselves: as well she might, Christa thought.

The glass appeared to be taking a rest. Linnet said politely, 'We're sorry about that, spirit of the glass. Have you any more messages?'

YES.

'Who is your message for?'

C-H-R-

'Linnet, I'll kill you for this.'

-I-S-

They waited for the short sideways move to T. It didn't come. Instead there was a drawing back and a move forward again:

-S-I-E-

'*Chrissie?*' said Linnet, clearly struggling not to laugh. 'Do you mean Christa by any chance?'

C-H-R-I-S-S-I-E, the glass repeated with precision.

Christa said hoarsely, 'That's me.'

'But Mrs Beresford,' said Linnet, 'who calls you Chrissie?'

'Nobody,' said Christa, 'since I was about ten.'

When Linnet and Dolina weren't born. When Ellen was a little girl up the glen. When Chrissie Forrest had come to stay in this house, helping and hindering the maids in this very kitchen. She closed her thoughts against the high clear voice in her mind: *Chrissie, where are you? Chrissie, come and get ready, we're going into the town.* Life had been full of instructions then, and at six, or eight, or ten, you followed them like a good little girl. *Chrissie, that's the tinks, they're dirty, come away.*

'What's the message?' she whispered.

After all this agonizing, however, the message, clear but incomprehensible, came across as YOU MIGHT COME AND PICK RICE.

'Garbled,' said Linnet with authority. 'Are you sure you're not resisting, Mrs Beresford?'

'I'm not sure of anything,' Christa said.

TIRED, complained the glass of its own accord.

'Spirit of the glass, do you want to go?'

YES.

'Thank you for all your messages.'

THANK YOU DEAR, said the glass civilly, moved back into the centre of the table, and went dead. There was no doubt about it: it was as dead as a broken-down television. They took their fingers off the rim and sat back cautiously; reluctantly. There was something missing in the room.

'Let's do it again!' cried Dolina.

'I'm not sure that would just be very wise,' said Ellen. She sounded quite worried, and no wonder; Dolina, hooked, was feverish with excitement.

'Oh, Mrs Macleod, you and Linnet never got a right message. Do you not want to ask it something?'

'You know it's entirely nonsense, Dolina. Isn't that right, Mrs Beresford?'

'Yes, it is,' said Christa. She was a mature and educated landlady, and that was what she was supposed to say; but oh, there was an emptiness in the room. The glass sat in the middle of the table, quiet, dead; but it had been alive. It had moved under their fingers, at its own will. Something, or somebody, not themselves, had been there, and could be there again.

Christa said with a laugh to show how little it mattered: 'I don't see any harm in one more turn.'

So gravely again Linnet washed the glass and breathed into it, as custom decreed. Funny how natural it felt already,

Christa thought, the awkward one-armed position, finger on glass, body bent slightly forward to follow the spirit's word. Of course it was only fun to them all, except perhaps Dolina. Of course Linnet had moved the glass. By no possible stretch of the imagination could the ladylike spirit of Aunt Sarah have been here, speaking in her kitchen to Chrissie her niece. Funny how you could actually feel the channel clearing, the mind lying open to whatever spirit might come. Open. Vulnerable.

Maybe it wasn't funny at all.

Dolina evidently didn't feel threatened: she was still riding high on excitement and thrills, looking forward to some more definite matrimonial advice. She giggled wildly as she put her finger on the glass. 'Here, wouldn't it be good fun,' she said, 'if we got a bad spirit this time?'

11

'Dolina —' they said, as one. (Only fun to us all, Christa thought in a blink of time.) They looked in real horror from one to the other. Ellen said, 'I think we should stop now.'

But the words had been spoken, and under their fingers the glass began to vibrate. They knew what the answer would be, but still Linnet said almost voicelessly, 'Spirit of the glass, are you there?'

With a great thrusting rush, totally different from the first spirit's hesitant delicacy, the glass said YES.

'Spirit of the glass, are you going to speak to us?'

A strong move across the table as if heading for NO. The answer turned out, unexpectedly, to be OK.

Ellen raised her eyebrows; but it was Dolina who leaned forward and cried 'Have you got a message for anybody?'

YES was the fierce reply.

'Perhaps it's a bit too soon to ask that,' said Linnet gently. 'Let's find out more about the spirit first. Spirit of the glass, are you a man?'

YES, said the glass. No one was much surprised.

'May we ask your name?'

Rather quickly the glass spelled A-D-A-M, and stopped with a jerk.

'Adam?' said Linnet. ADAM ADAM ADAM, said the glass in a bad-tempered way.

'Yes, all right, I'm Linnet.'

They gave their names. The glass waited under their fingers, trembling strong and angry with the power that wasn't theirs.

'Are you happy where you are?' Linnet said.

NO.

Ellen shook her head slightly with a worried frown. 'I

think we should get on and finish it,' she said.

Christa suddenly thought so too. 'Spirit of the glass,' she abruptly said, 'who is your message for?'

ELLEN.

'Is it a nice message?'

'If I may say so,' said Ellen with her eyebrows up, 'I preferred the last spirit we had.'

Without a moment's hesitation the glass replied FUCK YOU.

There was one indrawn breath around the table, then a shriek of horrified laughter. Linnet and Dolina had snatched their fingers away at the second letter, so that it was Ellen and Christa who unbelievingly found themselves spelling out the atrocious message. Ellen laughed as Christa had never seen her laugh before. Christa said 'Who – who – that's a bit much —' and Linnet cut across her with 'It wasn't me, you don't think it was me?' Dolina was speechless, rolling about on her chair. They laughed and laughed.

'Some people would say,' cried Linnet, 'that one of us was doing it subconsciously.'

'Oh, Linnet,' said Christa, 'which of us would have that in her subconscious?'

'Well, true enough,' said Linnet. 'I would just say it straight out.'

And, bemused with mirth, excited, quite beyond themselves, they settled their fingers on the glass again.

'Any more messages for anyone?' said Christa in a shaky voice.

YES, said the glass.

'Wh-who for?'

LINNET, rapped out the glass quickly, shooting about the table-top.

'Oh dear, is it a nice message?'

YES.

'All right, go ahead.'

Rather more slowly and with great precision, the glass spelled out: YOU ARE A BASTAR

Linnet, totally discomposed, shrieked and grabbed the glass. They howled with laughter. Ellen was trying to get out something which sounded, unbelievably, like a bawdy joke. One by one, shaking, their fingers went back on the glass. Immediately it shot across to D, and stopped.

'What?' said the shattered Linnet.

Ellen sobbed like a schoolgirl, 'He's finishing off the word!'

YES, said the glass triumphantly, and like a naughty child continued: CHRISTA.

'A message for me?'

VERY PLEASANT.

'Well, that's nice for a change, go ahead.'

BIG FAT ARSE, the glass blandly observed.

'That's very rude!' yelled Christa. They laughed till they cried. They wiped their tear-filled eyes.

'Oh dear,' said Ellen. Laughing, she was a different woman; her white teeth flashed like a tinker's in her brown face, her black hair stuck damply to her brow. 'Oh, Mrs Beresford, I think we should stop now, really. It's not nice this, not with the young lassies here.'

But their fingers were still on the glass, which went on as if she had never spoken: DOLINA.

'Oh no! A message for me?'

YES.

'Is it a nice one?'

NO.

'Then I don't want to hear it,' said Dolina with some pluck.

DOLINA, the glass said again.

'She doesn't want the message, Adam.'

DOLINA, the glass said.

Suddenly they weren't laughing. Ellen said, 'He's bound and determined, isn't he?'

'We should stop -' said Christa. She knew that they couldn't. Or Adam wouldn't let them; which? 'Well, we've all been sworn at except Dolina,' she said. 'I suppose he just wants to finish us off

'He needna think he's going to swear at me.'

'I tell you what,' said Linnet a bit anxiously, 'Dolina can take her finger off the glass and turn away.'

Dolina agreed to this, and so did the glass with an irritable OK. They spaced three fingers evenly around its base. It waited, throbbing with malevolent life.

'If it's more swearing, Dolina, we just won't read it out,' said Linnet, satisfied in her peacemaking role. 'Spirit of the glass, we're ready for Dolina's message now.'

The power gathered under their fingertips, and poised, and hung. 'Speak, Adam,' said Linnet encouragingly.

Clear, precise and wicked under their horrified eyes, the glass spelled out: DOLINA WILL DIE.

Nobody could have missed the shock and silence in the room. Dolina was turned half-round from the table, honourably following the rules. 'Well? What is it? What'd he say?'

Christa knew they couldn't tell her. There didn't seem to be anything else to say. The pause felt a million years long. It must have lasted for only seconds before Ellen evenly said, 'It was just nonsense, Dolina. Gibberish, that's all.'

'Garbled,' said Christa in a rush. 'Like mine about the rice, only more so.'

'It probably doesn't work, after all, if your finger isn't on,' said Linnet. Under the sweep of hair her face was absolutely white.

'Well, all right then, I'll put —'

Ellen said in her usual brisk way, 'Do you know we've never had any lunch and here it'll soon be dinner-time?'

'Yes, we'd better —' Keep it normal, was all Christa could think. 'Any more messages, Adam?' she said, dreadfully afraid.

NO, said the glass with a cross shove.

Linnet said carefully, 'Well, goodbye, and thanks for everything.'

FUCK, said the glass succinctly, and went dead.

No one had much good of the afternoon off. They tried to sunbathe, but the sun had long ago drawn round behind the house, leaving the garden cold and shadowed as if in an eclipse. Christa didn't look directly at Linnet for the rest of the day, and she certainly couldn't look at Dolina, who chirped about the place with exclamations of wonder until Ellen snapped her head off. They didn't have dinner, only bacon and eggs at the kitchen table, since Billy had seen off the whisky bottle and was fast asleep in front of the roaring television screen. Christa heard Ellen say to Linnet in the pantry, 'I don't think you ought to tell anybody about -' and Linnet's still shaken reply, 'Do you think I would?' Only when the two girls were washing-up did Christa, on the excuse of next day's housekeeping instructions, meet Ellen face to face.

There wasn't time for discussion. 'You were quick,' she said, 'to say what you did.'

'What other could I? Nobody should get that kind of news,' said Ellen, 'and herself, she'd have lost her head entirely.' She shrugged into her coat, which Christa had never seen before, for she hung it aloofly, the moment she came in, on its peg by the side door: a black mohair car-coat, far from new, rubbed shiny at collar and cuffs. 'The hellish thing is,' she said in her slow clear voice, 'it was true what he said.'

'*True?*'

Ellen in her dark coat was only a glimmer of pale skin

and bright eyes in the shadowed passageway, 'Dolina will die right enough,' she said. 'We will all die. Unless you have other plans. Goodnight, Mrs Beresford. Sleep well.'

Christa didn't sleep well at all, though Billy on the sofa possibly did. She twisted and sweated in the hot lonely bed, and she dreamed.

She was in a spider's web of corridors somewhere in the back of the house. There was someone half-seen going in and out of unknown rooms, someone strangely familiar, but not in a comfortable way. The figure turned, and it was herself. It looked at her and its expression changed. Utter terror spread over its face. Christa sobbed and cried, 'Then what's going to happen to me?'

She had scared herself awake, and lay shivering and crying, wanting Billy's warm enfolding arms. Billy was snoring drunk two rooms away. Much nearer — but where? — someone was moving in the house. It sounded to be in the dark back corridors that she had never yet properly explored. It couldn't be; it was one of the girls up and going to the bathroom —

A floorboard creaked. All over the house there were old floorboards: they creaked and cracked all the time. She lay in the airless dark and knew that she had never heard that particular jarring oddly-pitched noise before.

Only she *had* heard it before, she thought, waking again, restless, far into the night. 'Do you hear that, Chrissie?' her aunt had said. They had come out to the farm specially to let the little city girl see the harvesting, and not a detail was to slip by unremarked. She remembered eating tomato sandwiches, sitting on a tartan travelling-rug with the stubble pricking through to the backs of her bare legs. It was sweetly, crazily unlike the park at home: 'Auntie, I wish I could live here always,' she said. She remembered the men with their shirts off, brown as tinkers, and the hoarse cry of the strange bird among the stalks of corn. That was when you hardly ever saw a combine harvester, and when there were still corncrakes in the clean sunny harvest fields around the little town.

12

Bethia added a pound of steak to the chops and chicken in her overflowing bag and remarked, 'You'll not be going to the ceilidh, Calum.'

'Oh, I will,' said Calum. 'The meenister's to speak. I couldna hardly stay away.'

'But it's your day off,' said Kate Frizell, soft as a snake.

Nora Macnair was teetering about behind the counter, powdered as white as her coat. Calum compressed his lips and said, 'Now would there be something else the day, Bethia?'

Bethia looked thoughtfully down the sunny street. 'There's many a man in this town wouldna lower himself to carry a message-basket,' she observed.

'I'm not just sure that I like to see it,' said prim Kate, though she took a good look all the same. 'A bit lassie-like, my father would have considered.'

'Aye, there's no' much spunk in him,' said Bethia, wriggling comfortably in her well-served fat. 'Them wi' no family too, and there's been plenty o' time surely. I wonder is he a bit o' a jennywillock?'

'Oh no,' said Kate Frizell.

Under the incredulous stares of Bethia and Calum her face went scarlet in slow stages from chin to brow. 'I'll take half a pound of tomatoes,' she said.

'Nora!' ordered Calum.

'Oh, maybe that's too much —' cried Kate in alarm. 'How many in a quarter, Nora? Is that all? Well, maybe half a pound is right enough. No, if you could just give me three —'

Mrs Macnair, demoralized, dropped the whole box of tomatoes.

'I tell you what,' said Kate, 'I'll call in again.'

'Make it in the next three minutes, Kate, or I'll be closed,' said Calum; which wasn't at all like him.

Billy, patiently waiting in the chemist's doorway, was somewhat taken aback when a little fierce flying woman nearly knocked him into the window display, and the more so when she threw him, as she sped past, a look of the most withering contempt. 'What did I do?' he began to ask Christa, who came struggling out of the shop with her arms full; but he found he really didn't care. He caught her toppling parcels for her and held the shopping-basket steady, and looked down with affection at the top of her busy red head.

The bad time was past and done. She'd had a tough few days with visitors and staff, all in the thundery heat that had built up from the first fresh warm days of June, and she had kept her temper. He had actually seen her laugh once, when Dolina, asked by a guest for another potato, had set off for the dining-room with the potato, plain and simple, clutched in her hand. Christa had certainly sent Dolina whizzing back to the kitchen like a cat with its tail on fire, but then she had come into the owner's flat and laughed herself sick and silly, which had proved to be a very good sign. That business up on the hill, forget it, just one of those things; she'd been overtired and nervy, he shouldn't have tried. Jean Lambert stopped to speak to Christa, and Billy beamed at the plain plump little runabout creature. His contentment overflowed. It seemed only right that, however distant and tuneless, there should be music in the air.

'Oh, there's Alphonsus Macafee coming up from meeting the boat,' said Jean. 'Oh dear, he gets worse every year. I haven't been back to the campsite yet, Christa, but I don't suppose you'd have time now. How's it all going?'

'Fine, thanks,' said Christa with her long-lost cheeky grin. Not even a twitch at the mention of tinkers; whatever had troubled her up at the camp, that too had passed away. Billy was emboldened to put his arm round her, and the delicate wriggling movement she executed made the hair rise on the back of his neck. He slipped his hand shamelessly downwards, right there in full view of Jean.

And of half Finavay, because one o'clock Thursday had struck, and all the shops were closing down. Kate Frizell was flushed out of the chemist's and Bethia Gillespie emerged from the butcher's. Down the street with two shopping-bags came Ellen Macleod, who'd had the morning off. She hesitated as she reached Billy and Christa. One of our don't-know days, diagnosed Billy: whether Ellen behaved like an employee or a friend seemed to depend on the mood she was in.

No, one of our shocked days: what's got up our nose? He smiled benignly at Ellen. Wives don't get their bottoms tickled in broad daylight in Finavay town. We don't approve, I see. At least we are acting very strenuously to indicate that we don't.

Bethia and Kate, fortunately perhaps, had approached from the blind side. They stepped on to the pavement as Calum Macnair's old banger did a kangaroo jump out of its parking space, and Bethia purred 'I thought you would be away home by now, Jean.' And that's a sly bitch, Billy thought. Why should he think it just then? 'Lovely weather,' he remarked like a country squire.

'Aye, it's on the change though,' said Bethia, the fisherman's widow, with a matter-of-fact glance at the heavy sky.

'I see they're trying a Thursday for the ceilidh this time. You'll not be going?' enquired Kate Frizell.

'Certainly I will,' said Jean a bit curtly. She wasn't fond of these ladies, that much was clear.

'Och, why not indeed,' said Bethia, 'it will make a change for you,' and the weasel look sat sleekly on her satisfied fat face.

'There they come,' Jean said.

It wasn't as if you could miss them, with their withy baskets and their handcart, led by the piper, pacing slowly up through the town. His greasy cap was pushed back on his grizzled once-red hair and he had a three-day growth of beard. To his stiffly stained jacket and trousers he had added a moth-eaten Royal Stewart tartan scarf.

'They trace their blood back. I wouldn't say they're wrong,' Jean murmured at Billy's side.

As they straggled round from the quayhead in a disorderly rout, their marching tune modulated with many a wheeze and false start from 'Amazing Grace' to the famous 'Finavay Hill'.

'That would bring tears to your eyes,' observed Billy. Jean glanced at him suspiciously. Christa, for some reason, didn't seem to hear.

The tinkers' cart was piled high with rags and kittens and bundles and bare-legged children. The whole tribe looked dirtier down here than in the sunny wood, as if the bad opinion of the town clung round them like a cobweb, blurring their colour and their raunchy style. Billy saw how Bethia and Kate drew fastidiously back against the wall. What in hell did they fear, the respectable ladies of the town?

Fleas or germs or whatever, Christa didn't seem to feel that way today. She was almost pulling forward against his arm, looking with strange intentness from face to face. 'You're interested in the tinks, aren't you, Mrs Beresford?' murmured Ellen on her other side. Fair comment, Billy supposed. But no need, remarked a deeper part of his mind, to say it at all.

Two women were pushing the cart, and three or four more, one heavily pregnant, walked beside it with bundles on their shoulders and baskets on their arms. Hughie's sinister granny was among them, but down here in the town, away from the tents of her clan, she didn't pack the same charge. She seemed older and smaller, and Billy saw, as he hadn't before, the dirt-channels seaming the skin of her hard face, and the arthritic knotted knuckles clenched to hold the shawl under her chin.

Behind the carts slouched the men with their hands in their pockets. There was the red-haired guy who had spoken to Christa up on the hill, and he was favouring Christa with more than one look. She wasn't interested in him, nor even in the old witch-wife Theresa. She was staring in a worried way at the cart where the children milled and squealed.

'Hughie?' she said. 'Where's Hughie?'

Ellen said 'Is that the wee lad you saw up at the camp?' Christa didn't answer, or apparently hear. Well, she must have managed to talk about it to Ellen at least, Billy thought.

The children were finding the whole thing hilarious. 'Hughie!' they screamed. 'Hughie Toilet!'

The cart stopped, perhaps only to let the women rest. Theresa turned sharply towards it and excoriated children and women alike with an angry burst of the harsh tinker cant. From deep among the rags, as if waking from sleep, Hughie Macafee raised his sunburnt head. He was whiter in the face than Billy liked to see a child, and he smiled in a tentative way. On his round baby forehead there was a huge blackened bruise.

Billy thought detachedly that it was odd how they all left the next move to Jean.

Dumpy little Jean, hardly up to the shoulders of the rangy tinker men, stepped forward as if she was in outpatients' casualty. She tipped up Hughie's chin and gently turned his face to examine the bruise.

'What happened there, wee man?' she asked the silent sunny street.

The pregnant young woman heaved herself forward and opened her mouth, but Theresa's loud voice drew like a rasp across hers. 'He fell an' hit his head on a tree-trunk, nurse,' Theresa flatly said.

Christa gasped.

'Did he,' said Jean. She patted Hughie's pale cheek and stepped back from the cart. The group of tinkers relaxed, ready to move on.

'Weans is aye hurtin' theirsels, sure they are, nurse?' said Theresa winningly. Billy stared at her and couldn't believe in her, so ingratiating, grandmotherly, sly.

And Christa, taut as piano-wire in his arm, couldn't and wouldn't leave it alone. 'Is he all right?' she demanded. 'Jean, should he have an X-ray? Shouldn't he see a doctor at least?'

Jean hesitated as if choosing what best to say. The tinkers gazed at the sky and the chimney-pots, embarrassed or bored. Only the red-haired young man, Hughie's father, really looked at Christa; surprised, then amused, then something else again. Billy's arm tightened round Christa's braced shoulders. She didn't seem to notice, or care.

Why in the name of God should Ellen Macleod, silent as death at their side, both notice and care?

The young tinker man said earnestly, 'We'll get it checked for ye, missis. We'll take him tae the surgery right away.' His eyes narrowed as if he was going to laugh. They were Siamese cat's eyes, as self-centred, as brilliant blue. 'Will that satisfy ye?' he said.

Theresa said like a whiplash, 'Adam!'

Billy felt a shock go through Christa as if she had indeed been hit in the face. He didn't know what the hell was going on.

The tinkers had felt the shock-wave too. The two women leaned as one on the cart, the piper hitched his bag under his elbow, and in a moment the whole clan was on the move to the uncertain opening strains of 'Finavay Hill'. Jean stared after them, very perturbed.

'He probably did fall and hit his head.'

Billy found it quite difficult to get out anything at all. 'I don't suppose they will take him to the doctor,' he eventually managed.

'Unless it would be a witch-doctor,' said Ellen coldly.

Bethia heaved and puffed in motherly concern. 'Cruelty to

a wean! That's something I canna bear.'

'That's the wee lad that was kept in hospital so long,' came Kate's narrow, slippery, comprehending voice. 'They'll not be pleased at him, coming back all neat and clean.'

'An' wi' decent civilized ways,' said Bethia. 'Oh, they'll take it out on him. A child that's different, they'll no' can be doing wi' that.'

'Cripples and twins havena much chance wi' them,' murmured Kate. 'So I've heard my father say.'

'They kill them,' said Ellen starkly. 'I've heard it in the glen.'

'Oh, many a time I've heard it,' said Bethia. 'They're namely for that.'

'Namely!' cried Jean. 'It's no wonder if they are!'

Bethia and Kate looked at her in absolute amazement. Bethia flounced: 'You know best, I'm sure, nurse,' she said, already three paces down the street.

'Will you be at the ceilidh, Ellen?' Kate said over her shoulder, the better to snub Jean.

'No,' said Ellen. 'I have another engagement.'

In the long word Billy heard her soft glen accent, foreign against the broad Finavay voices that were harsh as the sea. She had matched them for harshness a moment ago, just the same.

Bethia said gently, 'Och, I know, it would be different with the old minister. You'd feel you would need to be supporting him. You'll pick up on things again, give it time.'

A very uncomfortable silence reigned when she and Kate had floated away.

Jean blew out her cheeks and said 'They can be right bitches those two. Excuse me, Billy, but they can. And it's no wonder the tinks have a bad name.'

Ellen said very clearly: 'There's no smoke without fire.'

She stood straight and stiff and her fine high cheekbones were patched with red. 'You know fine, Nurse Lambert, the way they are. Cripples and twins, anyone different, anyone weak. If they don't kill them, it's very sure they don't encourage them to live.'

Jean began to say something, but Ellen wasn't to be stopped. 'It's the way they are. They're animals just. They live in the dirt together and they're — they're entirely — they're —'

Randy as hell, thought Billy in a kind of amazement, is what you're trying to bring yourself to say.

'Promiscuous,' Ellen said. She swung on her heel, scarlet-faced, and stalked off down the street with her heavy shopping-bags.

'Jesus in the morning,' said Billy.

Jean's plain little face was screwed up and pink. 'Hard lines on her, losing her husband,' she said. There was something else on her mind.

Billy let go of Christa's shoulders and rummaged for a cigarette. 'The tinkers,' he said carefully, 'seem to get it from every side.'

He had never seen Jean so discomposed. She said, her voice shaking, 'It's awful the stories you hear —' She was biting her lip. She had held herself in before Bethia and Kate, but she had something to say and it had to come.

'I heard of another wee boy —' Billy offered her his cigarettes, but she waved them aside. 'His pal asked him,' she said, 'where his baby brother was. And the wee fellow, he was four years old, innocent — he said "He wisny thriving, so my faither slew him."' She pulled herself together with an effort plain to see. 'But that would be fifty years ago. Did I shock you, Billy?' she asked.

He saw himself, as it were, reflected in Jean's concerned eyes. He pulled himself out of the shivers: on the rebound he was unreasonably angry with Jean, for showing him a glimpse of a cold and unsuspected world. Angrier with himself, because in his selfishness he had forgotten all about Christa. She seemed to have got fond of that wee fellow. The bruise was bad enough. What on earth must she be feeling now?

But when he turned to her, she was somewhere else. She hadn't heard a word of Jean's horrible little tale. Her eyes were brilliant and her face was flushed, and she was wildly beautiful with an excitement not to be understood.

'Christa?'

She said as if in her sleep: 'That red-haired man. Hughie's father. His name's Adam?'

13

In the darkened back room of the Finavay Arms two little girls in kilts and white blouses were singing 'Crodh Chailein'. It was extremely odd to come from the soft June evening, still as bright as noon, into this dim and smoky and musical place: odder still, Billy felt that he had done it all before. He paused as his eyes adjusted to the half-light, and put his hand on Linnet's arm to let her know that he had stopped. Under the boyish rolled-up sleeve of her plaid shirt her wrist was soft and round, a young girl's arm.

Yes, school concerts, always in June.

In the darkened hall some unfortunate father had always settled comfortably and lit up before the janitor swooped. Coming in from the daylight car-park, usually with Christa, though not last year of course. And there his mind blinked; would it ever give up? Christa slim and quick and vivid, showing the awkward schoolgirls what a long way they had to go. Well, not all of them.

Should have spotted her, the little bitch, on the first day of term. There it went again, pointless twisting guilt, which he had thought long ago settled and gone. 'Nina Morris, Mr Beresford,' she had said with big anxious eyes, and nothing registered with him except, perhaps, what a nicely-spoken girl she was. There she came as large as life into his wincing mind, with her parents and the headmaster too, her hands crossed protectively over the grey school skirt which hadn't protected her as it should; all because he was going in again to a concert on a summer night with his hand on a young girl's arm.

'Should we wait for Mrs Beresford?' said Linnet. 'I don't suppose she'll be long.'

He had left Christa in her petticoat, brushing out her red hair so that it lifted and sparked in the threatening thundery air. 'Go on, I'll come when I'm ready,' she had said.

'No, we'll wait for you —'

'Go on!' she snapped. He jumped and obeyed.

'She must have had to park down by the quay.' It wouldn't do to stand there by the door much longer, jostled together as people went by. Linnet's hair was done up in a cheerful pony-tail not at all unlike Nina's, and she had stuck dog-daisies in her ribbon bandeau. 'There's Nurse Lambert on her own beside the band,' he said. 'We'd be safer over there.' Linnet, unsuspecting, laughed and agreed.

It wasn't too easy, however, getting across to Jean's side of the hall. People were really beginning to come in, since it was now an hour after the ceilidh's official starting time, and the bandleader in a mood of abandon had just announced Strip the Willow. 'Come on, boys, take the lassies up, it's not the week we're here for!' he called plaintively, hitching up his accordion. Billy realized that if he and Linnet crossed the floor at this moment, they would find themselves leading off the first set; which would greatly intrigue the town.

But there was a rustle by the bar, and Dolina in the flouncy glory of her party dress came out on to the dance-floor with a thin dark young man. Her arm was round his waist under the jacket of his blue suit, and, glancing round to see who had noticed, he looked both alarmed and pleased. 'So that's the famous Finlay!' Billy said in an undertone. He'd been seen at Glenrosa only in fleeting glimpses, sliding round to the side door to call on Dolina, making hurriedly for the gate when Ellen had had enough. If he didn't exactly look like the Casanova of Dolina's reports, he made a diversion at least.

'That's Finlay,' said Linnet with a grin.

'Why isn't he at the fishing like everybody else?'

'He has a groin strain,' said Linnet gravely. 'They put him ashore yesterday and he came home by bus. Dolina's been beside herself with joy all day. Giving the guests *handfuls* of mashed turnip.'

'Linnet,' said Billy sternly. Linnet giggled and perched one small buttock on the trestle-table behind her.

Goaded by Dolina's success, the girls in their flowery dresses had pushed and fluttered the big heavy-footed farm boys into place: two couples of bashful visitors were persuaded to make up the last set, and with a crash from the cymbals the dance began. It wouldn't be possible to go anywhere until the willow had been stripped.

On Billy's other side Calum Macnair's gravel voice said 'It's no wonder if he would have a groin strain.'

Billy looked at him in surprise, and then beyond him to his little thin wife sitting upright on a bench. She might as well not have been there. Calum was flushed and sweating slightly. 'He's one o' eleeven, did you know?' he said to Billy, man to man. 'It used to be the talk o' the town how old Alicky Gillespie never gied Bethia peace. Mind you, she wouldna have been pleased if he had.'

Billy stole a look at the glass in Calum's hand, which had scarcely been touched. He thought of several things to say, but with Linnet on one side and Mrs Macnair on the other they didn't have a happy ring. With considerable relief he saw, coming in at the door, a figure in sports jacket and flannels, a lumpy hand-knitted pullover and an aggressively open-necked shirt.

'Ah, Mr Macnair, I thought I would find you supporting the good cause.'

And that pillar of the kirk, ready a moment ago to luxuriate in the sex-life of the thirteen Gillespies, replied with winsome modesty, 'Ach well, meenister, when it's for the weans, what else can you do?'

They fell into kirk-session conversation. Billy ran his hand through his hair. Linnet at his side murmured, 'Was he trying to say that Finlay's a chip off the old block?'

'Linnet,' said Billy carefully, 'I don't know what he was

trying to say.'

'And you don't think he said it.' Linnet was too clever by half. There was thought behind her big painted eyes, and a bit of a scare too. Billy shook his head.

Behind him Christa said 'Let's go over and sit with Jean.'

She moved forward and stood beside him, looking regally round the hall as if she expected the audience to applaud. Oh forget it, all you little schoolgirls: she was on fire, wild and beautiful, there wasn't a girl in the hall who could hold a candle to her tonight. Billy said in delighted anticipation, 'To hell with Jean!'

Christa smiled vaguely at him, trying, it seemed, to bring to mind who he might be. Her eyes were too bright, her colour too high. 'Is everything all right, love?' he said.

'You didn't shunt the car, did you?' said Linnet rather pertly.

'I nearly ran over some tinkers,' said Christa. 'They were coming out of the pub, it wasn't my fault. But I waited with the car for a minute or two in case they'd come back and set about it. You never know with tinkers.'

Billy looked at her in real worry: that thing about tinkers, there she went again. She hadn't been right since meeting them in the town. Had the kid with the bruise upset her, or his forward father, or that peculiarly dreadful story of Jean's? Odder than all of that had been the snatch of conversation he had overheard in the kitchen before dinner. She had been speaking to Ellen, who seemed quite recovered from her own funny turn. 'It can't be the same Adam, of course,' she had said.

'What?' asked Ellen, understandably enough.

'That tinker, the red-haired one,' said Christa. 'His name's Adam.'

'Yes, Adam Macafee,' said Ellen in her superior way. 'Didn't you know?'

And Christa, almost desperate, though he had no idea

why: 'But it can't be the same Adam, can it, Ellen?'

'Apart from anything else,' Ellen had said, this time inexplicably, 'he isn't dead.'

She's in over her head, Billy thought; whatever the hell she's in. And she can't get out on her own. 'What's wrong, my darling?' he gently said.

There was another teeth-jarring detonation from the cymbals. The dancers fell back, laughing and sweating and happy. 'I see some chairs just beside her,' said Christa. She walked up the hall gracefully with her head held high, and there very nearly was applause.

Billy stalked along, hot-faced, three paces behind her. So that's young Mrs Beresford, she's a cracker right enough! And that must be her man . . . He burned as if the voices were real. I don't know what in God's name she thinks she's doing, and I don't know why she's doing it. But it's going to stop. Get her into a corner and face her, well away from Linnet and Jean, hold her there and have it out, the whole miserable thing –

He reached out and caught Christa's arm.

He meant her to feel his grip, to know he was angry: he didn't give a fuck if she had bruises to show. His fingers encircled her slim arm; he felt the sliding tendons and muscles, so easily damaged, the fragile bones below. He opened his hand and saw his fingermarks already flushing sorely on her delicate skin. In horrified haste he let go. And he had buggered up the move as usual, because she hadn't noticed anything at all.

'Hello, Jean, we're here at last,' she said, sitting down like a child reaching base in a game. 'Yes, Dolina and Linnet too. No, Ellen isn't coming, she's doing something else tonight —'

Billy silently went to the bar and got drinks for them all, a field in which his failure rate was not so high. 'I don't know what she does do — 'he heard Christa continue in a clear carrying voice, a gift to the ears of the town. They'll think she's drunk, he thought, if they are feeling kind.

'Some way to spend your half-day, Jean,' he said, passing the glasses round. Jean murmured something about the children and how she could hardly refuse. 'I wonder,' said Billy savagely, 'if there's anybody who really wants to be here.'

But when Jean was in the party, conversation didn't flag for long. 'Finlay Gillespie's a neat wee dancer,' she remarked. 'He should take off his jacket though, he's getting too hot. His father died of a heart attack.'

'Did he!' exclaimed Billy involuntarily, and felt, more than heard, the merest shimmer of guilty amusement at his side. Not the side where Christa sat. Well, to hell with Christa. He leaned over till Linnet's pony-tail was brushing his cheek. 'Don't dare to giggle,' he instructed her pretty pink ear. He squinted at his glass and realized that, in spite of having got a double to calm his nerves, he would soon have to visit the bar again.

He could already feel the drink in his head; he hadn't been in the mood for eating any dinner, in the heavy warmth of the dark old house, with Christa so jumpy and strange. He was at the stage where everything seemed pleasantly straightforward. He nodded at a passing reveller and commented to Linnet, 'He'll soon be absh'ly incapable. *Not* a very good plan.'

'No, I'm sure,' Linnet rather nervously agreed.

Jean was giving him a long crisp look. He sat up straight and said, 'I was jush -just remarking to Linnet, the priest and the minister are over there talking to Calum Macnair. They might get up with me for a barber-shop quartet.'

'You behave yourself, Mr Beresford,' said Jean, dumpy as Queen Victoria and similarly dressed. Billy grinned and enquired if anyone else was for a refill.

Dolina came strutting past with Finlay, smirking at Linnet who hadn't got a guy. A couple of Gaelic songs had been sung to polite applause: now a sandy-haired man in a shiny blue suit got up and launched into 'The Drunkard's Ragged

Wean'.

'He always does that,' remarked Jean. 'He can't be stopped. He's a man Maclean, an incomer, from Islay I believe.'

'Touch of the tinker about his cheekbones, wouldn't you say?' said Christa.

Billy said loudly 'Jesus wept', and went back to the bar yet again.

The recitation was drawing loud applause, especially from the porch, where the shyer members of the audience had retired in case they might be made to do a turn. Dolina and Finlay had disappeared out there, though not, Billy reckoned, on account of stage-fright. Calum Macnair was at the bar, fitting his great sausage fingers round a large glass of whisky and a small tomato juice. Billy squinted at him lovingly. In the clarity of drink he could see that Calum wasn't just the comic old butcher-boy he appeared. You'd be sorry for him if you understood. Only trouble was, and here you wished you had a slightly cooler head, you didn't know what you were supposed to understand.

'Whyncha come an' sit with us, Calum?'

Calum looked over at their group — Linnet alert and amused, Jean disapproving, Christa in her fiery trance — shook his head, and went off without a word. 'Be like that,' said Billy generously, and shouldered his way back. '*Sure nobody else is ready for a refill?*'

Linnet held up her almost-full glass and Jean just frowned. Christa didn't answer, or didn't hear. She sat up straight on her chair, turning her head with quick movements to scan the hall from side to side. Who the hell could she be looking for? Calum Macnair? Finlay? The tinker guy? It was like watching a sleepwalker: Billy's hair prickled on the back of his neck. She was absolutely ready and ripe; a touch and she'd fall. The clear sight of drink led him again where he would rather not go. She had closed her mind utterly to any idea that the touch might come from him.

A large lady in a white silk blouse and a tartan skirt came up to the platform, and the band sat back. Evidently more Gaelic singing was in store. She loomed like a double-decker bus. 'Anybody feel like some fresh air?' Billy said.

Jean said reprovingly, 'Mairead once went quite far at the Mod.'

Billy was very much afraid that this time Linnet's giggles were going to escape. He couldn't escape himself without total disaster: they were too far from the door. He turned his head away from the tempting sight of Linnet's bent neck with its duckling curls on the hairline, and looked sternly down at Christa. If the sight of him was like a cold shower to her, well, she could equally serve as a damper for him.

Only it didn't work like that, because Mairead began to sing.

The unemotional Jean gave a little gasp of pleasure as she recognized the song. 'Oh lovely,' she said, '*An Ataireachd Ard*', the mighty surge of the sea.'

It was indeed Gaelic and unaccompanied and slow, all of which he normally found extremely hard to take. It gathered its power from very far away, like the long reach of the breakers drawing in to the shore. It hit him where he lived. He was open for it, stripped by the night's sore memories and humiliation and anger and drink. The long surging phrases rose and held and broke like a turning wave, and in answer he stirred and rose.

He leaned back and slipped his arm round Christa's shoulders, and she half-turned her head towards him. She was stirred too, he could feel it, she couldn't help herself, as the deep elemental force in the music gathered and grew and rolled. Through his shirt-sleeve and the light stuff of her dress he felt the eager trembling of her skin.

He had done it, he and the song, he had broken through her strange mind-barrier: she was hot and ready, and so was he. The music rose to its inevitable, unbearable peak, and fell hushing like small waves on gentle sand. 'Feel like going home?' he said in Christa's ear.

She shivered from head to foot, violently, like a spurred mare. She pushed his cradling arm away. 'Leave me alone,' she said, 'you're useless!' On her feet, ablaze with a barren fire, she turned and found Linnet in her way. 'And you,' she said in a fury, 'take those silly dead daisies out of your hair!' She pushed through the crowd and was gone before anybody found anything to say. The band-leader, with considerable presence of mind, called for an eightsome reel.

There was frantic set-forming and instrument-tuning and chatter, nobody looking anywhere near Billy. He was looking at Linnet, and she after a moment raised her eyes to him. She was pink and embarrassed like a scolded schoolgirl. She held her orange-juice to her lips and her teeth rattled on the rim. As if he was doing it for a bet, Billy deliberately knocked off his scarcely started dram.

'Well, we both caught it there, Linnet,' he said.

Linnet was almost in tears. 'I don't know what's the matter with her!'

'Ah, women's troubles,' said Billy charmingly; and quite unforgivably, he knew, even if it had been true. Last year Christa hadn't come to the school concert, irritably saying she wasn't in the mood. He had gone alone in a bad temper, because she had been white-faced and shrewish for a week or more, and arrived late having stopped over in the pub on the way, and found Nina Morris of 5B all worried in the corridor behind the gym because her programme money didn't seem to work out right. Pink and tearful, afraid of reporting to the dragonish Miss Mariner, downy curls on her neck under the caught-up pony-tail as Mr Beresford helpfully bent his head with hers over the programmes and cash. It had been pregnancy sickness with Christa of course, and no sooner had it cleared up than he was in very big trouble indeed.

'Leave the daisies in your hair. They're nice,' he said. 'What about that breath of fresh air?'

14

Bethia knew the Finavay weather: sure enough, there was a storm on the way. Christa stood outside the hall with her hands pressed to her hot cheeks. The midsummer evening was never going to be really dark, but it was a threatening, heavy kind of daylight, and thunder grumbled beyond the town. Though she hadn't seen any lightning, Christa felt her hair rise on her prickling scalp.

Behind her in the doorway Nora Macnair's thin voice girned 'Ye said ye'd stay till the meenister had spoke. I thought at least ye'd stay for that.'

'He's no' to speak after all, Nora. Did ye no' hear him say? The committee thought it wouldna suit the night.'

'Oh aye,' she said. 'An' who's the chairman o' the same committee? Who but you!'

'You werena finding much amusement that I could see. I thought ye'd be just as glad if I took ye home.'

'An' you to go out as usual. Pity if ye would miss yer —'

'Are ye thinkin' o' gettin' into the car?' said Calum Macnair between his teeth.

Christa drew back out of their view, into the shadow of the building, as they crossed the street. 'A heller supposing he was a — a shopkeeper —' was what Jean had said, not talking about Calum Macnair at all. There you are, Jean, a shopkeeper indeed, strangely raised. What would the heller, the tink, be at in the thundery heavy night?

Above the disorderly grey roofs of the town Finavay Hill hunched its shoulders against the coppery sky. When she had seen him coming out of the pub, Adam Macafee hadn't been headed up the hill. It hadn't been anywhere near closing-time, but he had come quickly out, and stood for a moment rubbing the back of his hand over his mouth, and then set off lightly, almost running; not up to the campsite, but down in the direction of the quay. Wherever he had been going, very likely he was still there.

So I could go up to the camp, she explained to herself, and make sure that Hughie's all right.

She closed her eyes, shuddering, against the sight of his little white face with the massive bruise. Veronica wasn't fit to look after him and Theresa didn't care. And Adam, he was hard and ruthless, violent like a hunting cat. They merged in her mind, they melted together in her body, Adam the man and the rough exciting spirit of the glass. She felt a guilty pull towards the power that wasn't her own. I won't be able to sleep, she said, unless I know that Hughie is all right. She hurried to the car.

She stopped by the roadside some way before the gate. She didn't intend to be seen; far less did she mean to speak to any of the tinks. In this endless summer twilight the children would still be running about. She would see Hughie, and he would be all right. If she didn't see him? If he wasn't all right? She left the path and struck up over the green hill.

The going was terribly hard round the shoulder of the hill, among last year's brambles and this year's tough young bracken stems. She came upon a sheep-track, scarcely that, only wide enough for a deer's narrow feet or the shoulders of a slender fox; she followed it anyway, and by the time it was swallowed up by the bracken she was just below the rocky outcrop that sheltered the tinkers' camp. She made one grim scrambling attack on it, and fell on hands and knees, scratched and breathless, on the edge of the bluff. Behind her in a black sky the thunderstorm rolled round and round Finavay Bay.

The camp looked exactly the same. What did she expect to see? The children were certainly still around. A baby was nursing outside one of the tents, its young mother pulling the screen of her shawl round its busy head as three teenage boys came skylarking up from the path to town. The in-between children were running and shouting and screaming and quarrelling all over the camp. She couldn't anywhere among them see Hughie Macafee.

'Fine night, Chrissie,' said Adam behind her on the hill.

He had come up through the bracken like herself. He was carrying his jacket over his shoulder with one finger hooked in its torn collar, quite at home. *Turn away, Chrissie . . .* He stood casually above her, not with any threat, because, she knew, it was already done. If he was a hunting cat tonight, he had already taken his prey. The smell of sweat and smoke and whisky and green bracken off him was the smell of death.

'You killed him, didn't you?' she said.

'Who?'

'Hughie. Your wee boy. He was different,' she said, 'so you killed him.'

'You're daft,' said Adam, and nodded down towards the camp. The pattern of children had shifted and changed. Hughie was there now in his dirty red jersey, running and screaming with the rest. He tripped and fell and a long-legged girl heaved him up into her arms. Both laughing, they staggered off round the tents and were lost to view.

'Never seen him better,' said Adam. 'Did you?'

He came towards her, swaggering a bit, smiling, bright-eyed. He's bound and determined, Ellen had said. About Adam. Not this Adam. It was all the same.

'I thought you had killed him,' she said, moistening her dry lips.

'You canna keep away, can you, Chrissie?' Adam pleasantly said.

He went down on one knee beside her and shrugged his jacket off his shoulder out of the way. He knelt over her where he needed to be. With one hand he pushed her backwards in a practised fashion while the other hand got to work. He smelled of whisky and cigarette smoke, just like Billy.

There really was plenty of time to think. I could have stopped Billy at this stage. I shouldn't have started at all. Not then. Not now. But I didn't start it this time, she lucidly thought. I started it that time, when he didn't want to, and the baby died.

Adam's Siamese-cat eyes were narrow and wicked and blue. The throbbing thrusting force as he came down was urgent and uncomplicated as the power in the glass, fierce, impersonal, unsought. Keep thinking, it wouldn't do to feel. If Billy would – when I don't want to – but he couldn't, he's gentle, he's gentle, and so —

'I don't want to do this,' she said clearly at the last moment there was for thought.

'That'll be right,' Adam observed.

He didn't wait of course, just picked up his jacket and went loping down into the camp. She lay drowsily looking up at the strong curling bracken stems, brilliant green against the inky thunder-sky. Hughie ought to be dead, though, she explained in her head. That's what I expected, you see.

She turned on one elbow, peacefully comfortable, and looked into Dolina's shocked, amazed little round Dutch-doll face, framed in the bracken sterns not ten feet away.

15

Dolina pulled Finlay down the hill, excited though he was and protesting all the way. 'It's disgusting, so it is,' she gasped as they ran. 'Out in the open like animals just! And you would get all cold!'

'Would you?' choked Finlay, getting his trouser-leg caught up on the step of the stile.

'Well, you mightna, but I would.'

'Right enough,' said Finlay doubtfully. It didn't sound as if he had thought it very far through. If that wasna just a man for you, no consideration at all!

They were out on the road, running down towards the town. Finlay was making heavy weather of it and eventually they had to stop. They stood panting under a tree by the roadside. Finlay got his breath back pretty soon and he was all over her, right up her skirt, fair beyond himself with excitement. 'Och, come on, Dolina, what about it, what's the harm?'

'What about your groin strain?' But it didn't seem as if that was going to hold him back. 'Not outside,' she said primly.

'Can we go up to your room then?' He grabbed her again and held her up against him, and oh boy, he was excited right enough, nothing to satisfy him this time but the whole way. 'Mrs Beresford couldna complain hardly, could she now?' he cunningly wheezed into her ear, and him with the beer on his breath.

'Ach, Linnet's only through the wall —'

'Linnet's at the ceilidh, sure it won't be out for hours.'

It seemed as if she'd gone and given him a half-yes. He pulled her by the arm and they ran helter-skelter down the hill and up the chapel road to the side door of Glenrosa.

'In here?'

'No, Finlay, I never said, I never meant —'

'Och, Dolina,' said Finlay in desperation, 'you've got to let me, I canna keep it in!'

He sounded as if he'd hardly make it up to her room, and a terrible waste was going to occur. 'There's somewhere we could go,' she said, 'though it's all dark, there's no light —'

'Well, I didna bring my camera.'

It was all dark right enough and Finlay was pretty clumsy, but he certainly seemed quite relieved when he was done. 'That wasna bad, was it?' he said.

'Oh you! You're terribly bold!' But he yawned comfortably and turned over on his side, showing every sign of settling down to sleep. 'Get up!' she said in alarm. 'I'm no' supposed to be here. Mrs Beresford doesna even know where this place is.'

'She'll hardly bother us then,' Finlay reasonably remarked.

She got him off the bed at last and into the passage, where there was just a glimmer of light from a cobwebby skylight above their heads. 'For God's sake check yourself over when you get outside,' she hissed. 'You're likely no' decent.' The heavy swing door across the passage opened to her push. She managed to step over the floorboard that made such a devilish squawk, though Finlay stood right on it of course.

However there was no sign of life in the kitchen or the owner's flat, or up in the maids' rooms. Even if Linnet was back by now, she was a sound sleeper; she'd never heard Dolina creeping downstairs all those times, and if Mr and Mrs Beresford had ever heard the floorboard yelp like a frog in labour, likely they had other things on their minds. Dolina had only been after lemonade and biscuits at first, but she'd been tempted into that wee extra bit of exploration and it had fairly turned out worthwhile. After the first time she'd taken a torch. She knew the way pretty well by now, and she and Finlay didn't fall over anything much on their way to the side door.

'Och, Dolina, it's comin' down in buckets.'

It must have been like that for a while, though of course they hadn't been paying attention. The gravel drive was a swamp, the roadside gutters gurgling under the rush of the rain. 'Go on, you big Jessie, you'll no' melt,' she said, and pushed him out with a fine feeling of power.

He went, but right enough you could never trust a man: he whipped back in, all wet and cheerful, for a goodbye kiss. It wasna fair, that, because although he was finished for the moment, Dolina found to her surprise that she wasn't, not quite. She wondered dizzily if it would be worth taking him back through again; but she had been so firm about ejecting him that after the one kiss and cuddle he dived out into the rain and sploshed away down the road. She stood there half annoyed with herself; and what with the cool evening air, and her dress all damp and clinging from Finlay's monkey-tricks, she realized that she had forgotten to put her pants back on.

They were her best pair too, from the catalogue, embroidered with hearts and flowers. She was now thoroughly annoyed, but she couldna just leave them there. She went softly back along the corridor, into the kitchen, and through the particular door of all the doors, into the passage that Mrs Beresford, thank goodness, had never yet found the time to explore. There was only a broom-cupboard on the left and an old-fashioned pantry on the right, neither of them used or needed nowadays: straight ahead, as far as anybody but Dolina knew, a blank wall. Mrs Beresford didna seem to have the faintest notion about the extra rooms through there.

Dolina pushed hard once more and the tight-fitting door opened with a fuff of stale air. She dashed into the room they'd used, scooped her pants up off the bed, and came out with them dangling in her hand.

Calum Macnair was standing in the passage, shiny wet under the skylight's struggling gleam.

In real terror she gasped, 'How did you get in?'

'Through the back door,' he said matter-of-factly, jerking his head over his shoulder. It was pitch dark along there and she couldn't see any back door at all, but right enough, if you had as many servants as those rooms had been meant for, you would likely have a back door.

Anyway there he was. 'I came in out the rain,' he was saying, wiping the heavy thunder-drops off his bald head. 'I was going up – I was for visiting a friend, but I think she'll – they'll hardly be back yet. You sometimes canna slip away so easy from those affairs. I knew there was a door here an' when it came on to pour I just dodged in. You know, where the fence meets the hill.'

Dolina just shook her head.

'There's no' many that do, right enough.' He smiled broadly, enjoying her surprise. 'I laboured to my uncle when this extension was building,' he said. 'Ach, they never used half o' thae back rooms, never needed them. Old Charlie Forrest, Sarah's father, he thought he was God in breeks.'

If he didna shut up Dolina thought she would surely be sick at his feet. There he went blethering on, and the really important thing still to say. She couldna for her life get her tongue round it. She had to know. 'How – how long have you been standing there?' she whispered.

'Long enough, my lassie,' he said.

Oh Dhia, that was it then, and him an elder, he'd never let it lie. It would be all over the town and people having their laugh on her, and maybe she would need to get married to Finlay and never know if there might be —

Eerily, as if he had read her mind, Calum Macnair said 'An' wi' Bethia's Finlay? There's surely bigger fish than him in the sea.'

It was so unexpected she could only gape. His little brown eyes were looking her up and down. And true enough she wasna finished entirely, she felt that very strong; and here he was getting excited now, and she was standing in front of him in a dark passage with no pants on. Well, at least he didna know that. Oh, maybe he did. She hastily put her hands behind her back.

'Enjoy it, dae ye?' he said.

He spoke as if it was quite a normal thing to enjoy it, and he was the first person she'd ever heard speak like that. Suddenly she was able to say it out, what she truly felt: 'There's nothing else near so good!' she cried. 'I could do it all day long!'

'Could ye?' he said.

It was like a conversation in a dream; not quite a nightmare, but heading that way. In the stuffy passage the peaty damptweed tang of his jacket was very strong, and the oily smell of his sparse wet hair. He put his hands on the wall, one on each side of her shoulders, leaning towards her, not touching her yet. It wasna exactly the way they went on when they would be thinking of taking advantage of you, and she was puzzled, beginning to be a bit scared. His thick butcher's fingers, accustomed to death, spread strongly on the clammy plaster, just by her throat. His eyes were shining in the thundery gloom. She felt she was just on the edge of something big. Frightening; big. Exciting, though.

16

Christa's eyes were still closed and she felt herself gently swinging, easy, at peace, between sleeping and waking, night and day. She scarcely knew whether she lay in a bed or floated on a summer sea, or whose was the bare back that pillowed her drowsy head. She was calm, she was rested, she was healed.

A blackbird scolded outside the window as the threat of a hunting cat broke across its morning song. She came a little more awake and turned in bed, for of course she was in bed; of course it was Billy beside her, lying face down, sound asleep. He had been like that when she came to bed, and he didn't look as if he had moved all night.

She raised herself on one elbow and looked sleepily, blissfully around. The cool sea-scented morning air ruffled the curtains and early sunlight latticed the bedroom floor. As usual, Billy had stepped out of his trousers, pants and socks all in one go and left them lying on the carpet, with his shirt crumpled three feet away. There were one or two withered dog-daisies inside his shirt.

She shut her eyes and the drenching cold water broke over her head.

You can't go through the rest of your life with your eyes shut. It is half past seven, she said, so the thing to do is to get up. Next thing, get dressed. That can't possibly do any harm.

She got dressed, though she couldn't have said what she was putting on: if they were clothes she could reach without passing Billy's side of the bed, they would do. She gave her face a cat's lick and knotted up her hair, because all of that was routine, following step upon step. If she only took things step by step, she might get through the day. To put one foot after the other, also, you didn't need to think. Remembering was bad enough, and she had begun to remember when the blackbird screamed. Thinking would be more than she could bear.

She went into the kitchen, deliberate step upon step, and found Linnet, for once flushed and harassed, in the throes of cooking a dozen breakfasts on her own.

'Dolina isn't here, Mrs Beresford.' Her eyes were huge and scared, mascara all over the place: no time to take it off last night, eh, busy girl? 'I don't think she's even come in. Her bed's perfectly smooth.'

'Oh God, that's all we need.' Christa reached for an overall; making coffee, now there was something that didn't call for very deep thought. 'You should have come and wakened me, Linnet,' she said, already automatically at work.

'I didn't like to,' Linnet whispered.

No, I can see how you wouldn't, dear. Not quite as kookie as usual this morning, are we? Christa didn't say any of these things. She stood with bent head, measuring coffee; as she passed from one spoonful to the next, her treacherous mind opened the gates. There isn't anything to choose, she thought, between Linnet and me.

And Dolina . . . Where did she go, from the hill? What kind of a shock would that give a little girl?

Cheerful holidaymaking feet pounded the stairs. The front door opened and shut, and the morning jogger crunched down the driveway. He would want bacon, sausage and egg. Upstairs water was running, and the visitors were opening their curtains and breathing in the invigorating highland air, sparkling after the rain, scented with bracken and sea.

'Well,' she said, 'we'd better get them fed.'

And because it was the next thing to do, they did.

By the time Ellen came in at half past eight, breakfasts were being eaten in the dining-room, and duties reallocated in the kitchen to cover Dolina's work until she should appear. Billy came downstairs looking totally miserable; Christa could see he had a hangover everywhere that it could hurt, body, mind and soul. She hadn't time to do more than give him two aspirin. He sat down at the table and buried his face in his hands.

Christa leaned over to put the glass in front of him, where he'd see it when he began to come to. His light soft hair, sweat-darkened, was tousled and rough and needing a trim over the back of his bent head. She kissed the hollow in the nape of his neck.

He jerked his head up, looking thoroughly bemused, as if this wasn't at all what he had cause to expect. No, I know, dear, but you see, on one hand we have you and Linnet, while on the other . . . She tried the thing over in her mind, phrasing it first one way then another. A little more time needed here. Choose a better moment, there's bound to be one. We'll be together, just the two of us, and I'll say . . .

Chrissie, that's the tinks, they're dirty, come away . . .

Step by step, doing the thing that next came to hand, she and Billy and Linnet were getting through the day. No point in asking for much more. Odd in a way that Ellen Macleod should be the one who seemed slightly in the huff: when she saw Christa kiss Billy, umbrage had descended like thin and freezing fog. But that was nonsense, Christa decided as she moved, determined, blinkered, efficient, from sink to cupboard to stove. There wasn't time to spare any more thought for that.

In mid-afternoon, the slack time when thoughts could have come out of the closet and made trouble, a small child was obliging enough to lock itself in the bathroom. Its father was off on a fishing trip and its mother wasn't in very good trim for climbing through windows. Ellen murmured to Christa, 'She's nearly as pregnant as Veronica Macafee.'

Christa couldn't reply. The sudden twist in her belly left her shaking and sick. With all her strength she pushed down the thought that had surfaced: crushed it down, to be forgotten, totally ignored; and, bustling, went to fetch Billy out of the residents' lounge. He hauled the heavy ladder out of the shed and round to the bathroom window, but when invited to climb up it he turned green.

'Never mind, dear, thank you, we'll manage.' When he had gone sheepishly away Christa was annoyed to find herself saying to Ellen, 'He's always like that with heights.' Always, Ellen, not just when he's got stinking drunk and laid one of the staff —

'It's a pity Linnet's off this afternoon, it's a job for young legs.'

'I'll toss you,' said Christa gloomily.

But up the drive, like an angelic messenger, came a smallish figure in a splendid Fair Isle pullover, who made nothing of the ladder at all.

'I'm really grateful, Finlay.' He was polite, carefully dressed, combing back his dark hair that had got a bit ruffled as he crawled in through the bathroom window. Even though dinner was now looming and the potatoes had to be peeled, Christa had felt obliged to offer him a dram, which he didn't refuse. He'd never know how grateful she truly was.

Because as soon as she saw him the pieces of the Dolina puzzle fell into place. Where else would Dolina go but into Finlay's arms? Well, fine, faults on both sides; Christa smiled broad-mindedly at Finlay. He'd come no doubt with a face-saving message from Dolina, a headache, a tummy-ache, very sorry, back tomorrow. Least said soonest mended, Christa thought; we'll keep ourselves busy, take it as it comes, time's a great healer, soon she'll wonder if it ever happened at all.

The message was still hesitating on Finlay's lips: of course he'd never officially met Dolina's boss before. She helped him out. 'Apart from climbing up ladders,' she said, 'were you looking for me?'

His young bony face went quite pink under its seafaring brown. Since he came in, she now realized, his dark eyes had been searching, puzzled, around and about. 'I'm looking for Dolina, Mrs Beresford,' he said shyly. 'Is she no' due her time off about now?'

'She's not here. Where is she?' Christa wished Ellen hadn't said it quite so sharply, seeing the startled look on Finlay's face.

17

In the middle of Saturday morning, with rooms to be cleaned because some visitors were leaving and lunches to be prepared because others weren't, Ellen came into the kitchen and said 'Finlay Gillespie's at the side door again. Will I send him away?'

'Oh God, we can't very well. Does he still seem to be worried, Ellen?'

'He's fair in the nettles,' said Ellen. 'But he'll never feel easy with you. You know how the fishermen are. It's with you being a red-haired woman.'

'I can't help that!'

'Och no, it's just what Providence sends,' Ellen impassively agreed.

Finlay was anxious and embarrassed indeed. 'I just wondered —' he said. 'I thought you wouldna mind -' He wasn't dressed up today, but in his old jersey and denims; as if, Christa thought, he didn't really expect Dolina to be there.

'There's no sign of her, Finlay. No word either.'

His dark eyes ('the Armada, you know', Jean had once cryptically remarked) were liquid with concern. He stood there apparently unable to go away. Christa thought of the beds to be changed and the lettuce to be washed. 'She'll turn up, though. Relax, eh? She's bound to.' She's not worth all this fuss, was what hovered on her tongue.

Finlay got out some words at last. 'I'm wondering —' he said, and looked up at Christa like a frightened puppy. 'I mean I'm thinking — Maybe I would be the last to see her.'

It rang very ominously, like a phrase from a police court report. Christa said 'After the ceilidh.'

'Aye,' said Finlay. 'Though we didn't stay to the end. We went – up the hill —'

His voice trailed off. Christa couldn't think what to say, and Finlay didn't know where to look.

'I was with her for a while,' he said with care. 'But then we said goodnight at the side door here. It would be getting late by then. The rain had come on.'

Even after seeing Dolina she had stayed for quite a while, lying in the bracken, strangely comfortable, heavy, relaxed, until the thunder was overhead and the first fat raindrops persuaded her to move. She had driven home in the downpour: she hadn't seen Finlay, it was hard enough to see the road as the wipers laboured and stuttered on the streaming glass. She'd gone straight up to bed, where Billy was already flat out and sound asleep. She hadn't noticed the dog-daisies then. 'Well, I don't know, Finlay,' she said helplessly. 'If I hear anything I'll tell you right away.'

He still stood there, now looking straight at her with those big eyes in his thin Spanish face. 'I didn't see her,' she said. 'I didn't go up to her room. I never do. There wasn't any reason to go up that night.'

'You wouldna have been wanting to see her?' Finlay said. It certainly was a question. Christa didn't answer, and he went away.

And did the accused make any alteration to her routine at this time? Well, yes, m'lud, on Sunday she went to church. Which was not her normal custom? Not in recent years . .

But it hadn't changed a bit: not the dark pews, not the plain windows high in the wall, not the settling down for the sermon nor the ladies in their hats. Christa had found a hat of Aunt Sarah's in a forgotten hat-box in the wardrobe; it wasn't as bad as it might have been, just a cap of feathers, but when she appeared downstairs wearing it Billy's mouth twitched. He was being terribly good and remorseful, and so he didn't laugh. Christa's heart turned over. She wanted to go to him; she would have to tell him, she wasn't being fair –

She couldn't do anything, not with Ellen standing there.

'Have a nice time,' said Ellen with her eyebrows raised.

'I've been meaning to go,' she said, and knew that she sounded defensive.

'Why not?' Ellen was amused. Her bright eyes took in the unlikely hat, and the summer dress and jacket which Christa hoped might pass as churchgoing attire. 'The trouble is, it's not like the city, this town,' she said in her slow glen voice. 'People notice you, whatever you do.'

'Thanks a lot, Ellen,' said Billy, unexpectedly and quite savagely.

Christa went, all the same. Why not? She sat, head high, in Aunt Sarah's old pew, and she very well knew that she was noticed. Jean, coming in, gave her a brief smile, but that was all right. Bethia Gillespie, overflowing her place in the dark oak bench, noticed her in a different way. Finlay wasn't there; he had some sense; they'd all have been looking at him too, wondering if he knew . . .

Because Dolina's disappearance by now was known in the town. That was absolutely clear, in the prurient glances of Bethia, the upturned nose of Kate Frizell. And if they knew, so would Calum Macnair. And if the rest of the town wasn't fully informed, that would be attended to as soon as Monday's shopping got under way.

The sermon began and Christa did try to attend, but it wasn't possible. Somebody must know about her, where she is, why she went away . . . The heavy oak doors were closed. You didn't come late to church, or unforeseen, or unsuitably dressed. Deliberately, testing herself, she played out that imaginary scene: the doors crashing wide, the wail of the pipes, the tinks roaring disgracefully in, women and children and men, Adam striding ahead. How would it be? . . . Very, very deliberately she took it further in her mind, to the point she had always sheered away from: Adam's broken teeth smiling, his orange head haloed against the clear glass window, the hard pew under her back . . .

No stir. None. Well, fine, that's good. So I'll go home directly, she said, and tell Billy. No problem. The fever's passed. I'll be able to tell him now.

They've no shame, Chrissie . . .

Framed in the doorway, threatening, as solid as in life, Veronica's heavy fruitful belly blocked out the sunny sky.

On the steps afterwards Jean said 'Nice to see you, Christa.' She really meant it: no dark secrets or hidden thoughts for Jean. The minister echoed the sentiment, which was his job after all, and so did Bethia, though the way she put it was 'Och-an-och, Mrs Beresford, whatna surprise!' She was too big to be edged round; Christa was caught in the little group of dark coats and tweed suits and sensible hats. 'How did you enjoy the ceilidh then?' Bethia kindly enquired.

'Oh, it was — interesting. I left quite early though,' said Christa. She hadn't exactly meant to say that. Well, hell, she thought, Bethia knows by now. The whole town probably knows.

'I heard a lot o' people didna stay,' murmured sly Bethia. 'You left early yoursel', nurse, did ye no'?'

'It went on a bit late for me,' said Jean, on her way down the steps.

Calum Macnair said abruptly from his post by the door, 'It was far too hot in thonder. It wasna a night to be indoors at all. Mrs Macnair couldna stick it. We came away ourselves.'

'It got much cooler after the rain came,' said Christa. Everybody fell silent, waiting to see if she had more to say.

She escaped at last. It's simple now, and it's high time. Just walk up the road to Glenrosa and in at the front door. Billy will be watching TV. He'll look up, and he'll look guilty, and he doesn't have to. Just say, yes, simply —

Jean beckoned from the car and she said 'No, thanks, I — I feel like a stroll first.'

And so instead of talking to Billy in Glenrosa she found herself sitting on a bollard by the harbour, where the fishing boats bobbed at their moorings in their Sunday sleep. *Golden Harvest* lay next to the quay, *Girl Mairi* alongside; *Annunciata* and *Ceol na Mara* and *Margaret Ann.* Occasionally she had come down the quay with Aunt Sarah, but it hadn't been a relaxed kind of excursion, because of the ever-present threat from the crying seagulls overhead. 'It's supposed to bring good luck,' Aunt Sarah would say through clenched teeth, scrubbing at the shameful deposit and throwing the polluted handkerchief away. Giggling wasn't allowed. Back, stiff with embarrassment, to dark Glenrosa, where unspeakable things were never even hinted at, and so they didn't exist.

Christa tipped back her head and watched the wide-winged gulls drifting and wheeling against the sky. Their weaving flight was purposeful and sure. The gentle rocking of the boats calmed her, and the splash of tiny waves against the shining hulls, and the water-sliding light in the salty air.

'Any word, Mrs Beresford?'

'No, not yet,' she said with a sigh.

Finlay looked awful, unshaven and pale. Even someone less experienced than Christa would have diagnosed his trouble. As if in confirmation he said, 'I went out for a pint last night.'

'Yes, well —'

He was swaying on his feet: she thought he was going to fall on top of her. She got up from the bollard as casually as might be and strolled to the edge of the quay, as if to admire the painted name of *Ceol na Mara* and the gilt curlicues on the high seeking bow. Broken light on the water dazzled her eyes. She began to say, 'I'll ask around the town tomorrow ...'

The breeze fell calm and the dark water in a moment lost its sparkle, swelling deep and still. It was right at her feet as she stood on the coping of the quay. It sucked at the weed-green piles, lifting oily and strong, capturing her eyes. She leaned over, drawn by the secret power.

'I canna fathom it,' wailed Finlay at her elbow. He was keening like a seal and she shook her head to clear the irritating sound. 'All my mates,' he said, almost beseeching her. 'It was like as if they was all laughin' at me. I canna think why.'

He staggered on the edge of the quay and she grabbed his arm. 'Well, don't fall in, that won't help,' she said. She was cross as a toddler's mother; and with the same kind of relief, though she could hardly think why. The cool little wind, revived, slapped her hair across her face. She stalked up the quay and the harbour chuckled around her, bright and innocent, dancing the painted boats on its glittering skin. 'I'll ask around,' she said over her shoulder to Finlay. 'It'll be something perfectly simple, I'm sure.' The sun sparkled on the shut windows of the quayhead houses, dazzling her eyes.

By Monday morning, when she began her mission of asking around the town, she still hadn't talked to Billy. Well, three whole days and no word of Dolina; she made her enquiries faithfully, responsibly, as a concerned employer should. She had come back from the harbour and told him lightly about her church imaginings, as far as the opening of the door and the bursting-in. She had thought that she might find herself passing easily on, without trauma, to what had to be said. She came to a dead halt, nothing explained.

He waited. 'You wouldn't hear much of the sermon,' he finally ventured to say.

One blessing was that she didn't have to do much explaining in the town. 'It'll be about Dolina, Mrs Beresford?' murmured Miss Veitch in the chemist's. 'You'll be awful alarmed about poor wee Dolina,' mourned Kate Frizell. Sure enough, the town was in full cry. It hadn't had such richness on its tongue for a good six months.

Calum Macnair was somewhat withdrawn. 'I wouldna worry too much, Mrs Beresford,' he said. 'Dolina's a lassie that's well able to look after herself Jean wasn't so sure, and she produced a promising lead by remembering that Dolina had an auntie in Glasgow. From among her patients she even dug out the name and address. Christa phoned the auntie, but Dolina hadn't been seen there for over a year.

The minister, consulted as a last resort, asked whether Christa had informed the police.

At the counter in the police station she said wretchedly, 'I suppose I've been putting this off.' The sergeant said 'I wouldna worry too much, Mrs Beresford,' and the rest of his remarks also followed Calum's view. He wrote down all the details she could give, including what Dolina had been wearing. For some reason that question made her feel sick.

He studied his page of notes while Christa pulled herself together. He was broad-shouldered, no longer young, with blue seafaring eyes. 'She wouldna be the first lassie,' he gently said, 'who would think things might be livelier outside.'

'Outside?' said Christa to Ellen later on.

'It's the way they put it,' said Ellen. 'Outside the cosy wee town.' Her smile wasn't very pleasant. 'You can see what they mean, right enough,' she said.

By the end of the day Christa knew there was nothing else she could do. She sat down like a story-book detective and made a list of names and statements. It clearly showed that nobody knew where Dolina was. She tore it up and threw it into the wastepaper bin; all those people, all those words. Poor wee Dolina . . . I wouldna worry, Mrs Beresford . . . It'll be a year or more . . . They're laughing at me, I canna fathom why . . .

'The town's fizzing like ginger beer,' she said to Billy, 'and guess who's shaken it up?'

'And you an incomer,' he very tentatively said.

He had been treading so gently for the last few days. Things were not exactly normal, but in an odd way they weren't too bad. She said all in a rush, 'They're wondering what we did to Dolina to make her run away.'

Billy said gloomily, 'From the way they look at me, I think they think they know.'

And then he went fiery red and said 'Sorry.' She couldn't bear it. That was totally unfair.

'It's all right,' she said. 'You don't have to worry about that.'

'It's up to you whether you forgive me,' he had said, nearly in tears, after the terrible business at the school. She remembered that she had put her hands to her belly, just beginning to show gently round. 'I thought I felt the baby move,' she said. After a moment he had covered her hands with his.

Well, he was happy again now anyway, even though she knew it was still all wrong. And the answer came on Tuesday: to the Dolina question, at least.

18

The letter had clearly been held up by the vagaries of the weekend post.

'Dear Mrs Berrisford,' it civilly said. 'I am sorry things has got too much for me so I have went away. Yours faithfully, Dolina Macdonald.'

Christa, in an ecstasy of relief, showed it to Billy and Linnet and Ellen. 'Yes, but —' said Billy. 'No. Never mind.' Linnet looked it over carefully and said 'I think it's Dolina's writing all right.'

'Oh, Linnet, don't be so sensational.' But Christa caught Ellen's sardonic eye. 'I did wonder about that,' she humbly admitted.

Though at last she had something to tell Finlay, he was back at the fishing and she didn't know where his mother lived. 'Down by the quay somewhere,' said Ellen distantly. Ellen's house was at the quayhead, but she didn't seem to be on coffee-morning terms with the neighbours.

Christa went out in search of Bethia, and found her, as might be guessed, in Calum Macnair's shop. She proudly handed over Dolina's letter, and Bethia read it in silence, with Kate Frizell hanging over her shoulder following every word.

Then, while Christa waited for their exclamations of relief and joy, they read it again.

Kate, the lawyer's sister, spoke first. 'Things got too much for her?' she said. 'What would she be meaning by that?'

'Well, I don't know —' Relief and joy seemed slow to dawn.

'Went away. Well, it's a puzzle how she managed that,' said Bethia judiciously. 'The day after the ceilidh? Friday? She wasna on the boat that day, and she wasna on the bus, neither morning nor afternoon.'

'Oh, Mrs Gillespie, you can't be sure of that!'

But of course Bethia was sure. Finlay had come home from Glenrosa on Friday quite worried, so she had immediately put enquiries in hand; and her cousin's husband, who knew Dolina well, was the conductor on the Glasgow bus. 'Flora Ferguson's home, though,' Bethia added to Kate in a slight digression from the matter in hand. 'She came yesterday just. Thought there wouldna be so many on the bus, being Monday, I dare say.'

'Home! She's never!' breathed Kate. 'Is she staying in her own house?'

'Well, she is, Kate, though you'd wonder how she could. She's no' seeing people, she's shut herself away.'

'It's best if she can put it behind her,' said Calum Macnair roughly. He hadn't craned over to see the letter, and he didn't sound quite his usual urbane self. 'She's no' the first and she'll no' be the last.'

This seemed to offend, or anyway silence, both Bethia and Kate, and Christa tried to get back to the topic of Dolina.

'But the steamer, you couldn't possibly see everybody on board —'

'I did on Friday,' Bethia simply said.

Christa didn't even try to follow the whole story, but it was circumstantial in every detail. Bethia had been seeing off her sister-in-law, who was very nervous of missing the boat, and had dragged Bethia down to the quay before she was tied up hardly, and then Bethia had to hang about just in case there was an engine failure and she didn't sail. 'It's her age, I doubt,' said Bethia. Christa thought this referred to the sister-in-law, though she wasn't absolutely sure. In any case, Dolina hadn't sailed that day.

'Unless she went aboard in a suitcase like thon wumman the other week on the news,' Bethia added with some relish. 'Jointed like a chicken.'

Kate said 'Feech!' and even Calum indicated that this was going a bit too far. 'Maybe she hitched a lift,' Christa suggested feebly.

'If she did that, God help her,' said Kate Frizell piously, 'wi' the kind of folk that's going about nowadays. There's Flora Ferguson the living proof of that.'

'And she was sitting by her own fireside,'said Bethia, smacking her fat lips.

Christa got home with a splitting headache and a weary weight on her heart. She stood limply by the washbasin in the owner's flat swirling aspirin around in a glass. Billy stopped in the doorway, on his way to the television in the residents' lounge. He didn't say anything, and she answered, as you did in marriage: 'It's nothing, just the usual.'

She heard herself say it, and she saw herself standing there with the water-glass, watching the tablets as they fizzed and danced and sang. She put down the glass abruptly and said 'Excuse me a minute —'When she came out of the bathroom, Billy was as white as the wall. She went over and took his hands: 'Just the usual. It was due,' she said.

Relief and disappointment struggled in his face; and he didn't want to say anything, in case she was disappointed too. Oh, darling, she thought, when I do tell you the rest, that's a bit I'll never tell.

Dark and complete it came into her mind: now perhaps I needn't tell him anything at all.

Clearly he thought he knew what was wrong. 'Christa,' he said, 'she'll turn up. You know what she's like. There's no use worrying yourself sick.'

'I'm just so afraid —'She picked up the glass again, rubbing her finger round the rim. 'In case she's gone away somewhere ... and, you know, done something. She might have — have become unhinged.'

'Why should she? She seemed pretty firmly hinged, I would say.'

'She might have seen something,' Christa said.

When she didn't explain further, Billy raised his shoulders in a helpless gesture and went to watch the cricket. Christa went into the kitchen. Linnet and Ellen were sitting at the table drinking tea, which seemed to be their constant occupation these days. Even the kitchen was not so trim and inviting as it had been. When she opened a cupboard, there was just a hint of a nasty smell; you would almost say that Dolina's patchouli was still lingering in the air. I'm obsessed, she wearily thought.

She poured out a mugful of tea, but it was cold and stewed. The tea in the nearly full cups on the table, she now saw, had curdled as it cooled.

Ellen said in her even, considering voice, 'We were just saying, Mrs Beresford, that letter wasn't very much comfort after all.'

Christa took her mug to the sink and poured away the horrible tea. 'What I keep thinking about,' she said, rinsing and rinsing, 'is "Dolina will die".'

'Me too!' cried Linnet on a gasp, as if a gathering boil had burst in pain. They looked at each other, all three, and knew what they were all ashamed to say. Ellen lowered her dark eyes and studied the scummy tea in her cup. Linnet sighed and put back her floppy light hair and said, 'You don't suppose we ought to ask Adam?'

The name hit hard. It's over, it's over, she desperately said. Why should she feel there was some reaction from Ellen too? She was strung up, witchy, just the usual: 'The spirit of the glass, you mean?' she asked.

'Yes,' said Linnet in surprise.

Ellen said, 'Yes, that's right.'

The silence stretched out and out. The little round table tempted from the corner of the room. It wouldn't take a moment. It would be very, very unwise.

'I don't want to,' Ellen said.

'Neither do I,' said Christa. She reached up to the shelf of the dresser, where, jumbled in the second-best whisky tumbler, ready and waiting, lay the twenty-six letters and Yes and No.

19

Almost at once, as if it had been waiting for them, they felt the power in the glass.

'Spirit of the glass, are you there?'

FUCK YOU, the glass tersely replied.

Linnet sighed. 'Is that Adam again?'

YES FUCK YOU.

'Well, we won't get much out of him in that mood,' said Ellen.

'He's always in that mood,' said Christa wearily.

The glass didn't approve of this and began to run irritably round the table. There was no doubt it was Adam: they all recognized the strong wicked scarcely-contained force. Christa set her teeth and said to herself: It's all nonsense, it isn't true – But she sat there, waiting for a message, with her finger on the thrumming glass.

'Adam,' said Linnet, 'we won't keep you long. We only want to ask about Dolina.'

The glass stopped its angry circling and moved with purpose in quick definite thrusts. DOLINA, it said.

'Is she all right?'

DOLINA WILL DIE, the glass coldly said.

Christa found courage. She leaned forward, her finger trembling on the glass. 'Yes,' she said, 'we know she will. Is she dead now?'

NOT YET.

'Oh Mrs Beresford, you mustn't cry.'

'It's all right,' said Christa on a sob. Linnet's worried young face spangled in tears before her eyes. 'It's all nonsense anyway. Let's stop.'

'Thank you, Adam, and goodbye.'

But the glass began again to run round and round, fiercely,

almost out of control. They could hardly keep their fingers on it. They couldn't possibly take them off. Christa whispered jerkily, 'He's not ready to say goodbye.'

'Have you a message, Adam?' gasped Linnet.

ELLEN, said the glass.

'But I —' said Ellen, and said no more. Christa looked up startled at the note in her voice.

'A message for Ellen?' said the patient Linnet.

YES.

'You're pushing it, Linnet,' said Ellen abruptly.

'No, I'm not, Mrs Macleod,' said Linnet. Her clear young eyes rested thoughtfully on Ellen's white face. 'I never have.'

Ellen said very low, 'Go on then.'

'What's the message, Adam?'

FROM LACHIE.

Ellen said 'No —' but the glass was moving again.

LEG –

'Do you mean let? Letter?'

'I don't think so,' said Ellen, hardly to be heard.

The glass spelled out: LEG IT WAS MINE.

'Well, that doesn't make sense,' said Linnet, much relieved.

But Ellen snatched her finger off the glass and sat, head down, her hands clasped in her lap. 'Oh Ellen —' whispered Christa.

The glass was off again, now with only the two of them to guide it, if guiding it could ever have been called: FUCK FUCK BASTARD FUCK -

'Oh Linnet, what have we done?'

The glass stopped in the middle of the table, and slowly moved around, spelling: NOTHING.

Christa and Linnet sat frozen in their chairs.

Linnet said to the glass, 'Why do you keep swearing at us? We haven't done you any harm, have we?'

NO.

'Do you hate us so much?' said Christa. It was nonsense, it wasn't true, her mind said again and again; but disbelief had to wait on the message from the glass.

NO. YES. NO, the miserable spirit said.

Linnet leaned forward and said very gently, 'You can't help saying those things, can you?'

NO.

And then, not in reply to any question at all, the glass spoke quickly and clearly: VERY SORRY AM A BAD ROTTEN BASTARD AND A FUCKING —

It began to move round in circles again, small wretched circles of distress. Linnet said gravely, 'That's all right, Adam. We quite understand.' She wasn't speaking to the glass at all. 'We don't hold it against you. We — we hope things will get better,' she said.

Slowly and with apparent difficulty the glass spelled out THANK YOU.

Then: BACK DOOR.

Then it went dead.

Linnet and Christa sat back, white-faced and sweating. 'Back door?' Linnet said.

'Well, I don't know,' said Christa. Her head ached, her arm ached, there were tension pains across her shoulders and down her thighs. 'Sounds garbled to me. Like that message I had about rice. Or Ellen's "leg it was mine".'

'That wasn't garbled,' said Ellen tightly. She told them in a few words why. When she had finished, Christa silently swept the little paper letters together into the tumbler, and took them across the kitchen, and put them into the Aga, poking them down with fierce jabs into the glowing coals: second-best whisky glass and all.

20

Silly wee lassie, he thought; disgusted, but far more disgusted with himself. Oh, you silly wee bitch.

She propped the crumpled pillows up behind her so that he got a waft of hair-oil and heavy scent. His guts heaved and he turned his eyes away, but what he saw was the pink frilly hem of her short nightie and her dirty legs and feet sticking out below. 'Have ye ever washed since ye've been here?' he snarled.

'It's no' very easy.' She wasna caring a bit. She smoothed down the frills over her big young breasts. 'Did they no' wonder when you went in an' bought this?'

'What if they did?' he wearily said. 'I couldna hardly go up to your room. An' Mrs Macnair's wouldna fit.'

'No, it wouldna,' she said, quite pleased. Her black eyelashes fluttered and lay modestly on her round pink cheeks. 'That's another thing though. I'll be needing Tampax soon.'

He kind of half knew what she meant. 'Would that be a thing you'd get in the chemist's?' he cautiously asked. She dimpled and nodded. He yelled at her, because it was all too much: 'I canna very well ask Rose Veitch!'

'That's your problem, big boy,' she said, mock brassy. God, no brassier than she really was.

He took a deep breath. 'It'll no' do,' he said. 'I came tae tell ye that. It's bound tae come out an' it'll be me that gets the blame. An' it's no' even going the way it should.'

'God help me if it went any better,' she giggled, all coy.

'It's far too slack midweek wi' the fishing fleet away. An' the young farmers, they've got their own wee circle, I canna get the word round them, some way.'

'What about your Masons an' your Rotary?' she said with a long, deliberately insulting look. 'Or your kirk session?'

He hissed with rage. 'So I'm telling ye that's it,' he said. 'It's no' worth the risk. We'll have to stop.'

She leaned back luxuriantly on the grubby pillows and linked her hands behind her curly head. 'I'm enjoying it fine,' she said. 'I'm no' going to stop.'

He couldna believe it, the bitch. 'I'll tell on you – I'll tell —' But of course there was no way, without telling on himself. 'You're on your own then. Who'd bring your supplies?' he asked spitefully.

'Finlay's pals come in. I'd send word to him.'

'He's no' tae ken!'

'You're surely no' afraid o' Finlay?' She giggled again, eagerly picturing a punch-up; he saw it himself and shuddered. 'You needna worry about him. He's just a wee boy.'

She wriggled more comfortably into the pillows and held out her hands to him. Under the sugar-pink nylon she was all smooth hills and shadowy forests, though she hadna a brain in her head. Her nipples stood up like thimbles and she ran her tongue over her lips in a way she'd learned God knew where. What else could he do?

21

'Thursday,' said Christa. 'I should have known.' She stood irresolutely on the doorstep of Jean's cottage, high on the chapel road above Glenrosa, wondering whether to ring again. Jean's Mini was in the driveway, so she ought to be in: she wasn't noted for walking when she could drive. Perhaps the car had broken down. Perhaps she had gone out with a friend. But to add to the puzzle, all the blinds in the house were drawn down. It was Thursday, and Jean definitely wasn't at home.

Christa walked back down the path and sat on the drystone dyke beside the road, surveying Finavay below her in the flat evening light. I know Jean, she thought. I count her as my friend. I have no idea what she does on a Thursday.

The town lay closed within itself, hugging its harbour, self-absorbed and sly. I don't know what Ellen does on any evening, Christa thought. Perhaps nobody knows that. And I don't know what Billy's doing just now. Or what he thinks I am doing. Or whether he cares. Oh, God, she bleakly thought, washed in the sweet soft evening air above the secret town: nothing bad was going to happen here.

The worst thing, of course, had been the great reconciliation scene, with Billy so grateful for being forgiven. It was all wrong, she knew it as she went through the moves, and just when things should have come together she had realized that now it always would be wrong. He had stopped and looked down at her, a bit worried, and said 'What's the matter, darling?' And she — well, she didn't intend to go into that with Jean.

But she could have told Jean, for being with Jean was no strain, about the small things that were wrong. The smell in the kitchen cupboards, for instance, now unmistakably there and getting stronger by the day. They couldn't track it down.

Christa cleaned the cooker and disinfected the sink, scrubbing fiercely, glad of something strenuous and mindless to do. Linnet and Ellen cleared out the cupboards, though it wasn't three weeks since they had been stocked. They washed the floor repeatedly, kept the windows open all day, removed a stray pair of wellingtons to the garden shed. The smell got worse.

And the town was in a funny mood. Bethia Gillespie now didn't speak to Christa when they met. People stopped talking when she went into shops, giving the uncomfortable impression that they had been talking about her. Once or twice she had heard children jeering and calling 'Chrissie!' behind her back; she never had found out who knew that old, inelegant name, discarded at college, forgotten everywhere but here. Linnet, sent one afternoon on an emergency trip to the butcher's, had come back with the oddest story of all.

'The shop was empty for once,' she said, 'and the old guy -' she had never seemed so close to being shocked '— he asked me what you used Tampax for.'

'What did you say?' said Christa in horrified fascination.

'I told him,' said Linnet simply. 'But then he asked me if it made any difference to having sex. Well, I advised him to get on his bike. Mrs Beresford, do you think he's started the male menopause?'

And the big trouble that made these little ones sting: still no word from Dolina, two weeks after the night of the ceilidh. Ten days after the letter which hadn't cleared up anything at all.

So Jean wasn't in. Lovely evening. Hours of daylight yet. No hurry to go home, to the dark unhealthy house where she wasn't able to look Billy in the eye and never would be again. Christa turned away from the town and walked slowly up the chapel road, just like a visitor enjoying the good fresh Finavay air. Fortunate there weren't any other visitors out for a drive, she thought when she found herself at the top of the hill. She hadn't exactly been staying alert. She wouldn't have noticed if someone had come down the road in an articulated truck.

Up on the beautiful headland, where she had once wanted to be, there was a stiff wind from the sea, cold, eternal, strange. The plain red sandstone church stood matter-of-factly right at the end of the road. Our Lady of Good Counsel, its gilded notice-board said. Well, thought Christa wearily, I could do with some of that. The door was open. There were no railings or gates or steps. The road led Christa's feet inside.

To her horror there was some kind of service going on, candles burning, people in embroidered robes, a disorganized mutter of prayer. She wanted to go out again, but that would draw more attention still. She slid into the back pew, looking round nervously to see who had noticed her. Nobody even glanced her way.

It wasn't like a church at all. Cool light from the high blue sky flooded the vault of the roof, and slanting evening sunlight poured through the double doors behind her, open to the clear air. Up near the front, in a focus of brilliance, yet more candles were being lit by busy, skirted little boys. There was a smoky lead-pencil sort of smell and a murmur back and forth between altar and pews. Whatever was happening, it was restful. Christa propped her elbows on the book-board in front of her and rested her forehead on her clasped hands. Even if the tinks burst in, it would still go on, she sleepily thought.

Because the door stood open, they didn't have to burst in.

The rustling and wheezing in the aisle might not have disturbed her tired and pleasant trance, nor even the sudden twang as someone heavy bumped down on the kneeler by her side; but the smell caught her by the throat. Soft earth, wild garlic, sweat, ammonia, smoke; the young bracken on Finavay Hill curling strongly against the thundery sky. She opened her latticed fingers and looked sideways under her hands, the thump of her heart enough to shake the bench. Aloof and imperious, fixing her falcon gaze on the faraway priest with a disapproving air, Theresa knelt upright beside her in the pew.

Anyway, it wasn't Adam; because that's finished, she desperately said. Finished, forgotten, I never want to think of it again. Truly, she assured God, since now and here it seemed the right thing to do; truly I'll tell Billy, somehow, and then it will be quite finished, and I needn't care whether I ever smell that smell again.

Sweat and bracken and wood-smoke grained in the skin, overwhelming the murmurous scent of incense and the warm candle-breath: Theresa had turned her head and was looking at Christa from the heavy shadow of her shawl. Her lips moved, not in prayer. 'A word wi' you outside, missis, after,' she said. Next moment she was gazing down the church again.

Not finished, not finished at all. Christa in pure terror hid her face in her arms. No one noticed; or if they did they took it for devotion. Up on the altar, swathed in stiff folds of white and gold, the priest raised in his two hands a golden sun. A little silver bell rang urgently and long. Theresa ceremonially bowed her stern empress head.

Veronica was there too, half-kneeling in the aisle seat because by now she could hardly fit into the bench. Christa couldn't possibly get past that great bulk, even if Theresa had let her go. The service seemed to be over, but no one was in any hurry to leave. People nodded to each other, or spoke softly, or knelt on in prayer. Theresa raised her right hand and drew it from forehead to breast and from shoulder to shoulder. 'We'll go round the back,' she instructed Christa, while her knotted fingers delivered three devout taps on the shawl above her heart. 'Thae candle-eaters wad shit theirsel's tae get tae listen in. An' Veronica, keep you away till we're done.'

'I'll go an' light a candle,' said the obliging Veronica, and lumbered down the side aisle to where a madonna gravely smiled.

Round the back there was only air. The church was right on the edge of the headland, almost too close for safety, holding up its red sandstone cross over the quarrelling waters outside the harbour bar. There was a yard of sheep-bitten turf, a low dyke backed by a wire-mesh fence, and then only the bare rock tumbling to the sea. The brilliant air stung Christa's eyes and she licked salt off her lips. Theresa was like a standing-stone against the sky.

She can't do anything, Christa thought. There are fifty people round the corner of the church wall. I can walk away, join the crowd, go down the road, go home. 'What do you want?' she whispered instead.

Theresa said abruptly, 'Has he bairned ye?'

After all her numinous fears Christa felt the threat of a nervy laugh. 'No,' she said, 'he hasn't.'

'Are ye sure?' said Theresa, brisk as a health visitor. 'Have ye seen your monthlies since? If ye think ye're late, ye needna worry —' She had thrust one hand under her shawl into the folds of her greasy black skirt. In some invisible pocket there was a rustling and fretting, as if her fingers crushed dry leaves.

'No, it's all right,' said Christa. 'I've — seen them. It's definitely — I'm not —'

'Aye, well,' said Theresa. 'That's a' I wanted tae know.' The snapping black eyes searched Christa from head to foot. 'Not quite all,' the old woman deliberately said. 'Did he force ye or did ye let him?'

Christa took a deep breath. 'I let him,' she said.

She had no idea how Theresa would receive that. She wasn't prepared for a sigh of relief. 'Then ye'll make no trouble for us,' Theresa said. She took a corner of her shawl and fiercely, as if angry at their weakness, wiped her overflowing eyes.

Christa said gently, 'No, I can't very well do that.'

'Oh, ye'd wonder,' said the worried old woman who had been so terrifying and proud. She sat down heavily on the dyke. 'It's aye us that's the villains. They'll sit up an' beg for it, an' then they'll cry rape, an' it's bundle an' go, like there at the turn o' the year.'

'You left Hughie in hospital,' Christa said.

'It couldna be helped,' said Theresa hoarsely. 'The stupit bugger he took her in her hoose, an' that disna dae.'

They were alone on the headland above the wrinkled sea. Blue islands slept on the horizon and a belated gull swung calling overhead. The sweet air of evening was too gentle to dry Theresa's fiery tears.

'The polis came round,' she said, 'but I faced them oot. I says tae the sergeant, says I, "Dae ye aye keep yours in yer troosers when ye're oot wi' a lassie?" They hadna any evidence, an' they didna proceed, an' Adam got away wi't again. I leathered the erse aff'm, but bugger the bit o' use. He's got some ither wumman in the toon.'

She drew a big harsh sigh through her broken teeth. 'Whaur's thon stupit bitch?' she demanded. 'I didna tell her tae emigrate. She's maybe went behind the dyke. She canna hold her water comin' near her time.' The tears had dried, if those wildwood eyes had ever shed tears. Once more they scanned Christa up and down. 'But you'll ken that story, missis,' she said, 'for I can see ye've carried a wean.'

'Yes, I've — carried one,' Christa said.

'Aye,' said Theresa without expression. 'I lost two man weans afore Adam. God forgive me, but whiles I wish I'd miscarried o' three.'

Veronica, sure enough, appeared from behind a handy bit of wall. She was near her time indeed, a full-rigged ship, a harvest moon. She leaned back as she walked to balance her load. Theresa surveyed her sourly. 'It's tae be a lassie, madam says,' she remarked.

The baby humped and bumped under Veronica's drum-tight skirt. Christa, hardly knowing what she did, tentatively reached out and touched where the movement had been. For a moment she hung on the edge of the old horror and fear. Veronica smiled a lazy proud smile and put her hand over Christa's, pressing it to her belly, holding it firmly in place. Under her palm Christa felt strong life.

'God help the wean,' Theresa snarled.

The baby kicked and turned, compact and sure, eager to begin.

When Christa got back to Glenrosa the sky was flushed with good-weather pink behind Finavay Hill. There was going to be a sunset worth watching, and the visitors were grouped at the lounge window waiting for the show. Billy was lying on the back of his neck with his feet up on the sofa arm, while the tennis highlights pinged to and fro.

'Honey, would you mind coming up to the flat? I want to tell you something.'

It was the last step on a very long journey; or maybe the first. All the way down the chapel road, hurrying as the sunset flew its flags in the sweet evening sky, she had built up what she would say, and what he would say in return. I don't know why I did it, she'd say; at least I do in a way, but it's all over now. It started with losing the baby, she'd say. It was nobody's fault, I was mixed up, things weren't right between you and me.

And he would say –

Only he didn't.

He sat half-turned away from her on the sofa in the owner's flat with his arm along the back. His long fingers rubbed up the velvety pile, and smoothed it, and rubbed it again. He never took his eyes from this work, except for one startled glance when she spoke Adam's name. That made it easy in a way to get through her piece, but very hard to know what was in his mind. Well, it was a straightforward matter now of waiting for his reply. 'It's over now,' she said, with joy, with love. 'We can start again.'

He still attended with great care to the velvet on the sofa-back. 'I think not,' he said. 'Not just at the moment, at least.' That wasn't expected. That wasn't what she had pictured at all. As she hesitated, he added 'I'm going down to the pub. Don't wait up.'

He picked his jacket off the chair and went out, shrugging it on. There was a moment when she could have called to him, but then the moment had gone.

22

And I haven't touched a drop since the ceilidh, thought Billy sulkily. Two whole weeks and she never even noticed. Well, she'll possibly see a difference tonight. And I'll go home and I will – I'll – I will *humiliate* her. That's what I'll do. 'There's worse things than laying schoolgirls,' he remarked to Finlay, who stood next to him at the bar.

Finlay seemed a bit startled at this, and for some reason wary. Billy examined the statement and he could see a sort of ambiguity in it. He couldn't be bothered to explain what he really meant. In the relaxing atmosphere of a dram or three, the whole thing began to have its comic side. Big improvement on how it had looked as he drove grimly down from Glenrosa, cold and sick and hurt and clinging to the lifeline that this time it couldn't, it surely couldn't be his fault. Make it a dram or four, and maybe it wouldn't matter at all. 'Whatcha drinking, son?' he enquired.

'I wonder,' said the barman with the greatest civility, 'if the boy has maybe had enough.'

'And you wonder if I have too,' said Billy. 'Set 'em up, Joe.'

'Just take it canny then, Mr Beresford,' said the barman, but he set 'em up.

Finlay grasped his pint and said belligerently, 'Whatcha mean about schoolgirls?'

'Nothing,' said Billy. At the end of the bar, where five or six young fishermen stood, an expectant silence fell. Finlay had been standing with them, but as Billy came in he had broken away angrily and stumped down to order another drink on his own, while they yelled some kind of kidding remarks. He glowered furiously at them under his black brows.

Billy sighed. 'C'mon and sit down,' he said. They lurched into two chairs without spilling too much of their drinks.

They sat there with their elbows on the table, drinking with concentration. Billy felt that everything was set up for a heart-to-heart talk. Too bad neither of them seemed to have much to say.

He cleared his throat and said 'Shouldn't you be at the fishing?'

'It's my groin strain again,' muttered Finlay. There was an unexplained but quite definite ripple of laughter from the young fishermen. They were at the kidding again, nearly unintelligible with their chuckles and their broad Finavay voices. Calum Macnair, who had been drinking alone and morosely at another table, got up and went out.

'He thought you were laughing at him,' said Billy to the young men. It seemed a great discovery. He felt very pleased with himself and ordered another round.

'Oh we wouldna do that, would we, boys?' More laughter, the kind that had only been waiting for a chance to break free.

'He's away to buy a nightie,' suggested one of the boys. This went down very well.

'Don't be speaking bad of Calum! He's the most important man in this town!' They laughed like anything, though Billy couldn't quite see why.

When he put his mind to it, he wondered how they also came to be there at all, in midweek with the fishing fleet away. 'What's up with them, then?' he asked Finlay.

'Ach, belly-ache or a sore leg, it's any excuse.'

'We just hadna the strength . . .' said a feeble voice, at once swamped in a tide of cackles and ribald remarks. Finlay hunched over his drink.

The swing door flapped. The young men examined the newcomer, decided there was no mileage in him, and returned to their giggling and cryptic delight. 'Donald,' said the barman, clapping down a dram without waiting for instructions. 'You're late on it the night.'

'Oh by God am I,' said the man, unbuttoning his uniform jacket with a sigh. 'Oh, it'll be scanty herring when I get home. Ten minutes till I would be clocking off and didn't we get an emergency call. A tinker wife in labour up the chapel road.'

'They've surely moved their camp.'

'Oh, she wasna in the camp, allow her,' said the ambulanceman. He began to laugh into his drink. 'Out for a wee walk, I suppose, and did she no' land herself on the nurse's doorstep shouting hurry up, its head's stickin' out. Dhia, there's somebody looks after those folk right enough.'

'Nurse Lambert's door? Lucky —' said the barman, but he didn't get far. The young fishermen found this exquisitely funny.

'Wee Jean's door? Ringing her bell on a Thursday is it? Oh the cheek. An' her wi' her new frilly nightie.'

'No, no,' one of them kept saying, 'you're wrong there —' The others were too happy to hear.

'Aye, pink for a girl. The wife was lucky she got an answer at all. No wonder Calum couldna raise a smile. It wouldna be a smile he'd —'

'Now, boys,' said the barman, to no avail. Billy listened in mild astonishment as they developed their theme.

'Watch out, boys, he's frustrated so he is, he'll be up for a piece o' the action the night,' they cried. 'Oh that's hardly nice an' Finlay sitting there. It's all right, boys, sure he's got a groin strain —'

Finlay turned furiously to Billy and shouted 'See! They're a' laughing at me an' I don't know why!'

'I'm not laughing at you,' said Billy, focusing his eyes with an effort and smiling in an understanding and fatherly way.

Unfortunately that wasn't how it came across to Finlay. 'You're the worst o' the lot!' he yelled. 'If I ken naethin' else I ken why she ran away! You were havin' it off wi' her!'

'No, no,' said Billy, still only anxious to help. 'She wasn't my type.'

'What d'you mean *wasn't?*'

'I mean —' said Billy, blinking. Finlay seemed twice his normal size. He's very drunk, Billy wisely thought.

'There's mair to it, I said so —' Finlay was standing up, leaning on the table, yelling into his face. 'I kent she'd never — She wouldna just — You've done somethin' tae her!' He swung a punch that would have lifted Billy off his feet; however, he missed. Billy nevertheless fell backwards off his chair amidst considerable noise.

All the young fishermen rushed to restrain Finlay, which at first Billy found quite flattering. 'No, no, Finlay, you're wrong, boy,' they kept saying.

'Are you all right, Mr Beresford?' said the barman anxiously. 'He has drink taken, you see. Now Finlay, calm down, he's twice your age —' Billy began to feel the solicitude was being overdone.

'I'm all right,' he said slowly and distinctly, and with dignity left the bar. It was too bad that a dog was passing by on its own concerns just outside the door. Billy fell over it and hit his face painfully on a corner of the wall.

He was on his hands and knees in the gutter, but the thump had cleared his head a bit. He could feel his face swelling over the cheekbone, and his nose was streaming with blood. Down towards the harbour he saw a policeman. Drunk and disorderly, he thought, that's all we need. He pushed himself up and found a precarious balance on his feet, one hand on the wall.

The policeman was running. You don't often see that, Billy thought.

The ambulanceman had come out. 'Are you all right, Mr Beresford? Let's see your face —'

But he saw the running policeman too. 'There's something up,' he said, and set off down the street in pursuit.

'See what it is, lads,' pleaded the barman, gamely sticking to his post as his customers milled out on to the pavement.

Billy sat down on the kerb. No point leaving, he muzzily told himself, till they find out what's going on.

And so the few midweek clients of the Finavay Arms were the first to know that a woman's body had been found on the foreshore. Billy's stomach turned right over at this; but it was Miss Flora Ferguson (the word soon came through), who had never got over the horror and shame of being raped, back in January; by a tink, it was said, though she'd washed away all the possible evidence and no charge had ever been laid. The news was enough to sober anybody, and Billy got up off the pavement. His hands were shaking like an old man's. The way it took Finlay was that he suddenly vomited like a fountain all over the street, splashing everybody within reach with the detritus of six pints of heavy and the pickled herring at which his mother was such a dab hand.

After that they all went quietly home.

Christa had waited up, against instructions, and totally against her usual custom. Until he saw her expression he had forgotten what a mess he was in. 'Who socked you?' she said, apparently uncertain whether to laugh or cry.

'I fell over a dog.'

But that didn't explain why he was shaking so. He sat down again, before he should fall down, and told her the Flora Ferguson story. When he had finished she looked at him big-eyed, and then grabbed him, burying her face in his bloody, vomit-spattered shirt, as if she was diving into shelter out of a wild and dangerous storm.

23

What's that stupid lassie doing? raged Ellen. Half past eight in the morning and she's reading a book! And where the devil's Chrissie? 'Are you on strike, Linnet?' she evenly enquired.

Linnet giggled and swung her feet down from the kitchen windowsill. 'I've got breakfast already, and I've washed up,' she said proudly. 'They're all going to the lighthouse for the day and I asked them if they'd just have boiled eggs. Can't start the beds till they've gone —'

'But where's Mrs Beresford?'

'She's having a lie-in, I think.'

'You *think*?'

'I went up to the flat and knocked, but she didn't answer. So I thought, well, I'll just ask them if boiled eggs will do —'

Ellen chewed her lip. She could have slapped the unruffled child. 'You can't sit there,' she said. 'We'll have to get lunch under way.'

'Oh no we don't,' said Linnet with a comfortable grin. 'They've got packed lunches, they'll be out all day. Relax, Mrs Macleod.'

I never felt less like relaxing, you little bitch. He rolls along at one in the morning, as if I'd nothing else to do –

Which you haven't, have you?

She jerked her mind away from that thought. 'I'd better go up and wake her,' she said.

'I wouldn't,' said Linnet gently. Ellen took no notice, of course.

She knocked at the door of the owner's flat, but sure enough there was no reply. She knocked again, listening. No sound, no movement, and nearly nine o'clock on a working day. Where could they be? Well, he could be under a hedge drunk as a fiddler's bitch, and she — Ellen delicately turned the handle and opened the door of the flat.

On the far side of the living-room the bedroom door stood open. Oh, they didn't care. There was a litter of clothes on the floor. Ellen stood frozen on the threshold and saw, as Linnet had seen, Christa and Billy peacefully entwined and fast asleep.

She closed the door and, burning, went downstairs. Oh, she's got it all ways, it isn't fair! Money and education and a chance at a right job. And a husband. And any man she wants besides. Ellen stood outside the kitchen, her nails biting into her palms. 'What's up wi' Billy Beresford?' he had said lazily, rummaging for a cigarette, the yellow light from the quayhead lamps streaking the sweaty bed. 'I seen him at closin' time wi' a bloody nose. He'll no' be much use tae her the night.' A dirty chuckle in the darkness as he went on

The smell in the cupboards was worse than ever. Chrissie would need to see about that before the sanitary department did. Ellen thought about a quick anonymous phone-call, but brushed it impatiently aside. Madam wouldn't care, the way she was today. That wouldn't take the smile off her face. Something else would, though.

'Come on, the last car's away,' she said to Linnet. 'We'll get the beds made to pass the time.' Linnet looked a bit startled, and indeed she hadn't quite meant to say that.

Bide your time, Ellen. It's not the moment yet. Christa eventually came downstairs all rumpled and pink-cheeked. Looks as if he's recovered, Ellen grimly thought. 'Everything's in order, Mrs Beresford,' she said, efficient and reliable. 'Linnet and I managed fine. They're all away to the lighthouse with their packed lunches.'

'Thank goodness I made them up yesterday,' said Christa with a radiant smile. She wasn't even going to apologize. 'That smell, Mrs Beresford,' said Ellen, all worried; Christa looked at her benignly from the skies. 'Should we clean out some more cupboards, or do you think it's the drains?'

At least it was something else to pass the time. Christa sniffed about and warily opened a few cupboards, and admitted that she still couldn't place the smell. She didn't exactly think it was drains. Ellen touched in a little cameo of typhoid among the visitors, lawsuits, ruin. Christa, coming back with an effort to something near reality, said she would phone Nurse Lambert, who probably knew about drains.

Jean couldn't come round until after tea, but that seemed soon enough for Christa, floating through the day. After a scratch lunch in the kitchen Ellen and Linnet went to count out linen for tomorrow's new batch of visitors. Christa and Billy disappeared into the owner's flat hand in hand. Linnet, perhaps a little over-relaxed, dropped a carton of soap-powder on the stairs, and Ellen let her have it hot and strong. The moment was coming. What day had ever dragged like this?

But even Chrissie had to put her pants on some time and cook the dinner. Ellen, going off duty at five o'clock, stood in the passage slowly and luxuriantly pulling on her old black coat. Christa was singing in the kitchen, thumping the rolling-pin to and fro. That pastry will be like plasterboard, Ellen thought with the top of her mind. She curled her fingers into her palm as if Christa's heart lay in her hand.

'Likely he's never much use,' he had said. 'He doesna know what he's missing, the man.' The match sparked and flared on his stubbly cheeks and the mouth that drew back like a cat's. 'She's no' bad,' he said. 'A bit on the skinny side like yourself. Right wee acrobat though. Where d'you think you're goin'? The night's young.'

Billy was no oil-painting today, with the mess his nose and cheekbones were in to add to the normal puffy eyes. Christa evidently wasn't in a mood to look at the mantelpiece. Ellen treated him to a deliberate stare up and down his long body, which was stretched on the sofa, feet on the arm. 'Sorry to disturb you, Mr Beresford,' she said.

'That's all right, Mrs Macleod,' he said lazily. On the residents' television the tennis buzzed and twanged. 'Had a busy day?'

'Busy enough.'

She waited, relishing the moment, now that it had come at last. She sought for the perfect, absolutely right words, that would burn into his brain, that he would never forget, that would send him storming through to Christa and — and — Bring them on. Think of her and all she has, all she's done nothing to deserve. Here in her house, in her room, with her sofa, her television, her man —

'I wish whiles I'd had more of a sitting-down job,' she said. 'In an office maybe. I could have done it fine if I'd had the chance. I never had the chance.'

Billy cocked an eye at her over the end of the sofa. 'You've had it hard, Mrs Macleod,' he said.

That nearly put her off her aim; and as it was she hadn't intended to go girning about herself. It was Christa who mattered, Christa had sinned, Christa had to be made to pay. Maybe an anonymous letter after all? But then she might not see his face when he got the news. That would never satisfy the desire as it squirmed and twinged.

She gathered her strength. Oh true, she'd had it hard. It wasn't fair what she'd had to go through. And Chrissie Forrest with her white face and red hair, with her money and her diploma and her pussycat smile — It was coming, it was rising like sickness in her throat: the deep bad excitement, as every night when she heard him scratch at the door.

'There's something I think you should know, Mr Beresford,' she said. 'Your wife has been sleeping with a tinker. That red-haired one, Adam Macafee.'

Even as she spoke, she knew it wasn't going to work.

His puffy face never flickered. 'Oh, I know, thanks, Mrs Macleod,' he said. 'She told me, you see.'

She drew in her breath with something like a scream. 'It's not fair!' she hissed. 'She's got everything! She's never had to want! She's got the education, I never had the chance, I'm every bit as bright, I only needed the chance —'

Billy stood up, long and tall. He's angry, I've made him angry at last. But he's not angry with her. It's me, he's going to take it out on me — And if he does? What if he does? She stretched herself towards him, arms flung back, open to all he might do.

He crossed to the television and changed channels with a thoughtful and concentrated air. She heard her own voice in ranting echo: what she had said, what she hadn't meant to say, the meaning he had picked up that lay like coiling marsh-gas behind the sore plain words. A golf-course filled the screen, brilliant green by a bright blue sea. He delicately adjusted the colour up and down. The camera panned round to a wooded glen, very like her childhood glen.

She was in no state to look out for traffic, and in the main street Calum Macnair's old banger nearly ran her down. He braked and solemnly waved her across. Thin little Nora sat by his side, looking straight ahead. The oddest couple in Finavay, but a couple all the same: paired off, thought Ellen savagely as she strode down to the quayhead. As God made you he matched you, her granny used to say. Till death do you part was the other saying you got flung at you. When you were made and matched and death did part you, then let the old grannies search their proverb-stores.

And it isn't fair, not fair, she thought, brushing her black hair with fierce angry strokes till it lifted and crackled in the silent room. Those two up at Glenrosa, he's never off the bottle and she sleeps with a tink, and there they are today like bride and groom. We never carried on like that, Lachie and me. We hadn't time. The brush lay heavy on her lap and she stared at her wedding-ring. Two years, hardly that. Then the storm. And then nothing, except that horrible call from the police out of the blue on an evening in spring. She couldn't give them the certain answer they wanted to tidy up their files. A leg in a seaboot: who could say for sure?

Only the spiteful, miserable spirit of the glass; whoever he was, or she.

The scratching came to the door, as she expected, pretty late. He'd been to the pub first. He knew she'd be here waiting. There was nowhere else for her to go.

She raised her head wearily and pushed back her hair. 'Aye, come in, Adam,' she said.

24

Well, so she must keep it in her room. Home early on Thursday for once, because of that tinker trollop and those buggers in the pub, and there she'd been scuttling in and out with that nesting look on her face. Aye, nesting! The only nesting she'll ever do, poor bitch, thought Calum, moving his hands and feet like a robot, nursing the old car home. What a home, what a car! The town had him named as a miser, fine he knew; the same pokey terrace house all his married life, running a car that wee boys pointed at in the street. A man with his own business, sure it's thousands he'll have in the bank! I wish to hell it was in the bank, he bleakly thought. It's no good to man or beast where it is.

You could only fiddle the books so far, and the other scheme wouldna save him, never, never. His stomach turned at the memory: the wee slut lying there on her dirty pillows, costing as much as she earned besides. I'll need tae put my foot down, he said, as he had said so often before. He stole a sideways glance at Nora, sitting like a dressmaker's dummy in the passenger seat. Well might she sit straight, and her corsets stuffed rigid with ten-pound notes. I'll have them off her, he thought in a slow and growing rage. In hell's name, I'm her man, am I no'? Her wasted fingers with the broad gold band plaited and twisted in her lap. Was it rage he felt at all? It wasna her fault he'd started going with Jean when she'd lost the urge, years and years ago. It wasna exactly my fault either, he dared to think; but he knew all too well what the town would say about that.

But she needna take my money. Surely to God it's time I put a stop to that. He nursed the anger as it strengthened and grew. He parked the car anywhere and followed her up the front path. He was at her heels when they went into the living-room. He stood by as she took off her rat's-tailed fur-collared coat. She glared at him, but what could she do?

'I'll need to go to the lavatory,' she said, all lumpy and bumpy under her dragged-on woollen dress. 'Will you let me by?'

'Are you not well, Nora? You went before we left the shop.'

She shot him a look of icy hate and whipped into the bedroom instead. She banged the door and he heard the feeble little bolt snick home. He gave her one minute exactly, picturing what she might be doing, and then he kicked the bolt out of the frame. She had started to dig in under her corsets sure enough, though she hadn't got far; she was bending over like an old man's nightmare, with her dress rucked up and her drawers pulled down, hauling a suitcase out from under the bed.

He pushed her aside and grabbed the case. It was a small cheap suitcase, not old, and when he clicked it open it was three-quarters full of fives and tens. Coldly as a doctor he thought: And then there's today's. He seized her skinny wrists in one broad hand and pulled her to him, pushing the other hand up under her corsets. He felt crackling banknote paper, and slack old skin, and wiry hair. 'Oh no, Calum, no, no, no,' she whined. He was shaking so much that he could hardly close his fist on the money. He pulled it out and dropped it on the floor like clots of dunghill straw.

She lay sprawled on the bed still whining, she'd never stopped: 'Leave me some, oh leave me some,' she begged. He heaved himself off her and started to gather up the scattered notes. I'll leave her some and shut her up, he thought, kneeling to scoop his share from the little case. He saw another case, a bigger one, under the bed. He lay flat, huffing and panting again in black parody of what he'd just been at, and reached in among the dust and scurrying silverfish. There were three big cases in all.

He closed the last one and stood up, dusting off his knees. He picked up the small case; Friday night, there might be a pound or two to add. 'I have some business to attend to,' he said formally to Nora, and went out.

He never took the car to Glenrosa, because there were always eyes to see where it was parked. Anybody seeing him, he thought as he stumbled up the road, would imagine he was drunk, not just in despair.

25

'It has ripened considerably,' said Billy, 'even since this morning, wouldn't you say?'

'All the easier to trace it,' said Jean with professional cheer.

Christa opened a door or two, sniffing cautiously. The smell was everywhere, penetrating, vile. 'It seems to be in the cupboards,' she said, 'but you can't go by that. When somebody burns toast down here you can smell it in the linen-cupboard upstairs.'

'I see,' said Jean gravely, as one who had heard it all before.

She went round the kitchen sniffing into cupboards, examining the skirting-board, poking about in the sink. 'I don't think it's drains,' she said. She opened a door and the smell grew stronger, definitely nearer at hand. She shut that door and opened the next one, and the smell hit them full on. Billy turned away hastily, clapping his hand to his mouth.

'Needn't ask you to change the baby's nappy,' said Jean cheerfully. She closed the door and Billy, wiping his brow, lit a cigarette. 'There's your trouble, Christa,' she said, like a plumber.

'But that leads to the back of the house somewhere.'

'Well, that's where the smell is,' said Jean patiently, 'and I think it's something decomposing.'

Christa felt the blood leave her head and her skin go clammy and cold. Billy's hands on her shoulders pressed her into a chair; Jean's matter-of-fact little hands pushed her head towards her knees. 'No, no,' Jean was saying, '*not* Dolina. More like baked beans.'

Christa's eyes cleared and she said 'I never really thought —'

'I could tell that,' said Jean drily. 'No, it's —' She paused, anxious to be accurate. 'Corned beef, that's nearer it.

Somebody's too lazy to walk to the dustbin, Christa. They've been throwing your tins out of the back door.'

'But we don't use tins!' cried Christa in wounded pride.

'More to the point,' said Billy gently, 'we don't exactly know if we've got a back door.'

Jean looked at them in amazement. 'Well, we'd better find out,' was all she eventually said.

They went out by the side door: so far so good. On their left the path ran plain and unmysterious to the side gate. On their right there was no path, just a line of slabs hard up against the wall of the house. There wasn't room for more: the back of the house undercut the hill so far that it was nearly in a cave. 'Who built this extension? Your grandpa?' said Jean. 'He should have been shot. I very much doubt if there's even a damp-proof course.'

They followed the slabs round in single file, Jean first, as if being a nurse conferred immunity to whatever might be there. The smell grew stronger, unbearable. 'Breathe through your mouth, Billy,' said Jean. They turned the corner of the house and found a dank, dark little area under the dripping face of the hill, floored with greenish, slippery slabs. Blowflies rose buzzing from the pile of unwashed tins, and there were maggots too. Christa was the one this time to retch and turn away. She found some shelter inside the open back door.

The passage was almost totally dark, just the dim light from the door where they stood, and a glimmer from a dirty skylight farther ahead. Somewhere along there, something was going on: creaking of rusty springs, panting, a giggle. Christa looked up at Billy and badly wanted to giggle herself at the expression on his face.

Jean wasn't amused. Even in the half-light it was plain to see the angry flush on her plump cheeks. 'We'll put a stop to that!' she said as she made sturdily for the source of the sounds.

'Easier said than done,' murmured Billy, following her in.

Christa had the impression in the gloom that there might be several rooms off the passage, but one was clearly their goal. A line of light defined it, thin and bright around the shape of the damp-warped door. Through the chink an increasingly urgent rhythm thumped and plunged. Without consultation they paused outside the door. Even Jean, presumably, felt it might not be quite the moment to burst in.

Indeed it was difficult to know exactly when they should burst in, so that they were still standing there when the door opened, spilling warm light into the dirty dark. A young man in a fisherman's jersey strode out, zipping his denims with one hand and digging out money with the other. He was looking in the opposite direction down the passage, so that he didn't see them where they stood.

He had hospitably left the door open and everything in the room was in plain view. In the light of the storm-lantern by the big brass bed Dolina was peering into a handbag mirror, the better to arrange her hair. She sat naked in a jumble of crumpled sheets and grimy blankets, though a sugar-pink frilly nylon nightie flaunted itself over the bedside chair. The room smelt heavy and damp and grim. She had done her best with the patchouli, however, which almost overwhelmed the stink of the rotting meat.

They were all standing in shock; as once before, Christa and Billy found they were looking at Jean. This time she didn't respond. 'Donny Angus Macrae,' she said. 'I delivered him.' She was staring the same way Donny Angus was looking, towards someone at the far end of the dark passage, someone who had perhaps hoped he wouldn't be seen.

Over her words Donny Angus said cheerfully, holding out the money: 'Here y'are, Calum boy, your turn now.'

Calum Macnair came along the passage roaring, in ruin and unexplained.

The startled client looked about him in horror and shot out of the back door so violently that the air was left vibrating where he'd been. Calum Macnair paid no heed. He might not have seen Christa and Billy and Jean. He pitched forward into the dirty room like a diver, with his arms stretched out, all his body following his twitching, crooking hands. He fell on top of Dolina, knocking a gasp from her; she even gave a kind of hopeful laugh, but there was no lust in his mad eye. Nothing but death. His fat strong fingers fastened on her neck, and as she thrashed and struggled under him his broad thumbs seared into her gulping throat.

Ahead of Billy, far ahead of Jean, Christa flung herself into the room. She yelled desperately, impotently, throwing herself on his bull's shoulders that were hunched solid in their frenzied intent. 'No!' she screamed. 'Dolina's not to die!'

26

It was a terrifying scream. Billy, half-way across the room, saw Calum's head jerk up; in a moment he had his hands on Calum's wrists. He knew at once he wasn't strong enough: there wasn't a chance of breaking that grip. He thought of choking Calum, smothering him, but he couldn't get at the blankets. Just then Calum shook his raised head, as if to clear the jangling echoes of Christa's scream. His fingers slackened on Dolina's throat.

Billy pulled Christa up off the bed, even gave Calum a helping hand. 'Put your nightie on at least,' he said, tossing it over so that it half-covered Dolina's sturdy legs. She sat up like a dazed kewpie doll in the pink froth of its frills.

He heard Christa draw a deep breath. She had decided it was a moment for the garment of efficiency: thank goodness that she had. 'If Dolina gets dressed,' she said, 'that will be something,' and, beckoning Jean into the room, she stooped over the terrible bed.

Billy took Calum by the elbow and steered him into the passage, where they stood in the struggling grey light. Billy hadn't the slightest idea what to say.

Calum said, nearly shouting: 'I was needing the money!'

'Yes, Calum, sure, I know.'

'You dinna!' yelled Calum. 'You couldna! Naebody knows! It's her, she takes it all, she's bled me white!'

'Who?' said Billy cautiously.

Calum was off again. 'I knew those rooms were there an' I knew you didna know. What's a few extra rooms tae you?' He was sweating terribly and his face was like lard. 'I laboured tae my uncle. I nearly built this house. I could buy it now if it wasna for her!'

He swooped and bent double; Billy thought he was going

to collapse, but he was only lifting a small attache case off the floor. He balanced it on his knee and thumbed desperately at the catches. Pound notes, fives, tens, even a twenty came juddering out as the case shook under his trembling hands, sifting down to be lost in the shadows of the dirty floor. 'That's just the wee case,' he said. 'She's got three big ones under her bed.'

No use trying to make sense of him. Whatever he wanted to say, it wasn't coming through. He was a disgusting fat old man. The frenzy had gone and he was in a lather of wretchedness and fear. 'Come and sit down, Calum,' Billy said. 'It's not as bad as that.'

He turned to go out again by the discovered back door. Behind him Calum said in a small voice, 'Quicker this way.'

They appeared to be walking into a blank wall, but in the wall was a close-fitting door, heavy enough not to have warped with the damp, that opened with a puff and a wheeze. 'Jesus wept,' said Billy. 'The proverbial baize door.' There was no answer, of course. He meekly followed Calum, who was plodding on like the master of the house indeed. Along another bit of passage, through a door; into the familiar everyday kitchen of Glenrosa. The smell that hung about it seemed only a rumour when you remembered the stench at the back door. Calum sat down heavily and laid his case of money on the table, as if that was somehow supposed to explain it all.

'There's about two hundred pounds still floating around the passage,' said Billy.

Calum screamed, 'There's thousands o' pounds under her bed!'

Billy poured a dram for each of them. He made his own a double, and Calum's, on reflection, rather more than that. Calum gripped the glass in his trembling fat hands and gulped it like hemlock. 'That's it then,' he said through his shivering. 'It'll be a' over the town by morning. We'll need tae pack up an' go.'

Standing drinking with Calum: it had happened before. Billy's thoughts struggled to come clear. Looking with a drunk man's insight at a fat old butcher, known to the whole town, a pillar of the kirk: 'They'd be sorry for you if they understood,' he said.

Calum slammed his glass down so that whisky jumped and spilled over his hand. 'Then they're no' to get to understand!'

In the silence the fire in the Aga, banked low for evening, sputtered and glowed. 'It's nae use,' said Calum. 'She'll let it a' out now.'

'I'm not sure that I would,' said Billy, 'if I was her, I mean if it was me.'

'The young fellows then. Sure they're hee-hawing a' round the pubs already. They'll never keep it in.'

'Who'll believe them?' Billy said.

The kitchen clock ticked, one, two, three, as Calum's heart beat in his quivering fat throat.

'They believe anything in this town,' Calum said, 'be it true or no'.'

'I think that's what I mean.'

Calum tentatively reached out for the bottle. 'It wasna such a bad plan,' he said. 'You must admit you hadna a clue. An' it's no' as if she minded. God, it's what she was made for, her.' A flicker of pleasure crossed his face. He splashed his glass full in three jerks. 'There's her,' he said, timing the words to the spasms, 'an' there's the lads. But I would always be wondering about yourself.'

Billy thought clearly at last: This is an evil, amoral old man. He's spotted me as a soft mark. He is going to play me like a violin.

It took both of Calum's hands to hold the glass steady. They shook as they had shaken on the suitcase full of banknotes, strewing two hundred pounds disregarded on the floor. Then

Calum had locked the case; if he had shut any secrets in there they were locked in, as surely as he was locked into the narrow box of the town.

Billy breathed in and out, a long sigh. 'They'll not hear it from me, Calum,' he said.

Calum buried his nose in his whisky glass and drank off what was left like spring water. The thin strands of his grey hair, worked loose from their careful placing across his greasy scalp, fell across his brow, and he put a hand to his temple where the great vein throbbed. Miserably he said, 'It'll never work.'

Hughie Macafee's round pale face with its cruel black bruise. The baby under his palm, turning and kicking and near to birth. Christa's slim arm, crushed if he had closed his fist: 'Let's try it, eh?' Billy said.

Calum pushed his glass across the table for a refill. Billy seriously measured out another thumper and watched him knock it back.

'In the morning you'll wonder if this ever happened,' he said. 'Away you go home and have a good sleep.'

'But how can I sleep,' said Calum, 'wi' her counting her money next door?'

Jean was standing in the doorway that led to the dark passage and the forgotten rooms. She was dumpy and plain as ever: Queen Victoria to the very life. Calum looked across the kitchen and answered what she didn't say.

'Aye, well,' he said. 'If you wouldna mind.'

27

Billy and Christa came down into Finavay on Monday to attend to a few everyday pieces of business, like paying the butcher's account. On the short road from Glenrosa it didn't take long for the little toy town to grow life-size, standing round them grey and calm, window-curtains fluttering in the salty breeze. Behind the curtains, people who knew Christa. Well, Christa knew a few of them now.

'They used to look coldly at us because we'd mislaid Dolina,' she said. 'Now it's because we've found her and we're turning a blind eye.' Oh, never again, please God, a conversation like that, in the thick mingled smells and the shaking lantern-light: Dolina all remorseful at the terrible thing she'd done, namely, being found in a part of the house where she wasn't supposed to be.

'It's not as if it would help anything,' said Billy absently. His arm rested along the back of the passenger seat as he reversed into the last parking space on the quay.

'And she doesn't want to go away.'

He completed the manoeuvre before he said 'She'd still be Dolina, whether she goes or stays.'

She felt the tense muscles of his arm across her shoulders: he was waiting for her to make the connection, and spark, and flare. She leaned back and turned her cheek to rest on his hand. They hung in a bubble of peace. Never mind the windows. Never mind the town.

'Anyway we need her so badly,' she said, drowsy and content, 'with Ellen going off sick like that. When Ellen comes back, then I suppose —'

'I don't think Ellen will be back.'

She craned round in amazement. He grinned a bit too jauntily, as if he'd said more than he meant to, and leaned across to open her door. 'Why on earth not, honey?' she asked.

'Just something she said.'

Christa got out of the car under the eyes of the town. The fresh breeze fell slack. The window-curtains settled in their folds, closing the secrets in.

But there was Ellen, perfectly normal, walking straight-backed from the quayhead up the street, with an unmysterious shopping-bag on her arm.

'Oh, Ellen, how are you now?'

'Much better, thanks, Mrs Beresford,' said Ellen with her half-smile.

'Will you — did the doctor —'

'I've got a few more days at home yet.'

Christa said hastily, 'Don't come back till you're quite fit-'

Ellen inclined her head, collected and calm. Oh, she was an anchor, she was a rock: a landmark in Finavay's twisting narrow ways. 'But get fit soon. How could I get along without you?' Christa said.

'Oh, don't worry, Mrs Beresford. Trust me.'

She was making for the butcher's. Christa's gaze followed her fondly as she glided in, and rested her shopping-bag on the counter rail, and stood looking from her superior height over the other customers' heads. Calum Macnair rolled forward, merry as ever, bending towards the waiting women with what was evidently one of his famous jokes, though Ellen didn't seem to be amused.

Christa said in a kind of wonder, 'He has got away with it.'

Billy didn't disagree.

'Because if anybody knew, those ladies would.' Fat and thin, broad and narrow, their heads drawn together over a delicate morsel of news: peeling a secret, not reaching the core. She shivered, and Billy said gently, 'Why don't we go home?' He held out his hand, palm upwards, for hers.

Across his words struck the high and strutting strains of 'Finavay Hill'.

The tinkers came round into the main street, led by the piper, with their carts bundled high, tent-poles and bags and tarpaulins and babies. Veronica sat on one of the carts nursing a baby with a fluffy coronet of orange hair. From under the shawl waved its tiny arm, in a shop-bought nylon cardigan of triumphant pink. The children ran yelling alongside, and Hughie Macafee with them, happy as a king. Theresa bawled at them in the rapid incomprehensible tinker tongue. Long ago in the sunny town, a thin satisfied voice: *Feech, Chrissie, it's the tinks, thank goodness they're moving on.*

They didn't have the old van. It's beaten Adam, Christa thought quite calmly, even amused. They've just left it up on the hill. It will sink into the bracken, birds will nest in it, perhaps they'll get it fixed next year –

Adam was walking behind the carts.

She would have to look at him for the first time since that night, and he would look at her. She set her teeth and lifted her head, ready for his answering eyes.

He did look at her. At, or over, or through.

His snake-blue eyes were perfectly blank. He didn't remember. He doesn't even recognize me, she thought. I was — I was only — The coarse words jumbled in her mind as she stood with her hands pressed to her face. Mrs Beresford, Christa, Chrissie; he didn't care and didn't remember, any more than the tom-cat remembered the last squirming tabby but three.

Up and down the main street the curtains stirred and then hung still. I don't know the town, she thought. I never will. If I leave tomorrow, no one will notice that I've gone. Billy and Linnet, and Dolina, and Adam; ripples on the bay. The dark still water lifted and fell below in its powerful deeps.

'I think we should go home,' said Billy. He bent his head and kissed her in full view of the town.

28

Kate's thin fastidious voice scraped in the heavy air of the shop: 'Feech, it's the tinks, thank goodness they're moving on.'

'Well they might move on,' Bethia said, folding her lips above her triple chin.

'I wonder,' said Calum, though not with much enthusiasm, 'who'll get her house?'

It won't be you, you old skinflint, thought Ellen. Living like a pauper and you with thousands in the bank! She looked aloofly out of the window, up the sunny street, and picked her words with care. 'There they go, the two of them,' she said. 'I wonder how long they'll stay.'

Kate said almost in awe, 'That's a terrible word that's going around the town.'

'It's a God's blessing Finlay had the sense to break it off wi' that wee hoor. And he did it long ago,' said Bethia, quite as if she expected to be believed. 'I can see the way you would feel you couldna stay on there, Ellen.'

'Well, it's not exactly what I'm used to.'

'I'm sure it's not the sort of thing we're accustomed to at all in this town,' said Kate in well-practised disdain. 'I canna hardly believe it yet.'

'Oh, it's true enough,' said Ellen. Christa and Billy drove past, making for Glenrosa, just time for a quick bit before tea. She waved a gracious hand. 'I believe she'll be for it,' she said, 'her and her man both. There's word they'll be had up for keeping what's called a disorderly house.'

The oohs and aahs and twitters from Bethia and Kate were satisfactory indeed.

Before their startled eyes Calum took off his butcher's coat and laid it aside. He leaned his heavy forearms on the counter as if to stop himself falling down. There was glistening sweat on his pale fat face and down in the hairy notch of his open shirt collar. He gave a sigh. 'It wasna exactly like that, ladies,' he said.